The Actor

also by Robert J. Conley

BACK TO MALACHI

The Actor

ROBERT J. CONLEY

Doubleday

NEW YORK

1987

Library of Congress Cataloging-in-Publication Data

Conley, Robert J.
The actor.

1. Cherokee Indians—Fiction. I. Title.
PS3553.0494A64 1987   813'.54   87–13482
ISBN: 0-385-23956-4

for
Jan D. Hodge

and for Gerald Gladney,
whose invaluable suggestions
for reshaping made this a much
better book than it would have
been without them.

Author's Note

The Actor is a work of pure fiction. However, the character Bluford Steele was suggested to me by a number of very real historical Cherokees. Early in the nineteenth century several Cherokee families were sending their sons to northeastern colleges and universities for an education. In the 1820s Buck Watie, later known as Elias Boudinot, and his cousin John Ridge were sent to Cornwall, Connecticut, and the Cherokee interest in education continued strong until 1907 when the new state of Oklahoma confiscated the entire Cherokee school system. Another Boudinot, using the stage name of Frank Star, became a professional actor in New York City in the second half of the nineteenth century, and his son followed in his footsteps, using the same name. There were also numerous Cherokee gunfighters on both sides of the law: Cherokee Bill, Ned Christie, Samuel Sixkiller and Henry Starr, to name a few. Blue Steele, then, is simply an amalgamation of several different, quite real human beings.

The Actor

CHAPTER ONE

Bluford Steele stepped out of the carriage in front of Booth's Theater in New York City. With a dramatic flair he threw his black cloak over his right shoulder, reached for his wallet, took out a bill and handed it to the cabby.

"Keep the change, my good man," he said.

"Why, thank you, sir. That's a generous tip."

"Use it to buy a ticket to the play tonight."

"What's the play?"

"King Richard the Third by Shakespeare."

"Oh," said the cabby, scratching his head, "I don't know."

"If you don't, you'll pass up a chance to see the latest dramatic sensation in his first starring role."

"Oh," said the cabby, showing some slight interest, "and who would that be, sir?"

"Me, sir. John Berringer Temple. Good day to you."

Relishing the sound of the invented name, Steele as Temple strode toward the theater. He paused at the entrance to enjoy once more the playbill which prominently displayed his alias. He was early and so had time for such indulgence. He knew that he would have many successes in the future, but never again would there be such a night as this—this night of the emergence of a star. He postured there before the poster and began to read every word from the top line.

BOOTH'S THEATER

MANAGER . . . . MR. E. BOOTH
STAGE MANAGER . . . . MR. J. G. HANLEY

8:00
FRIDAY EVENING, JUNE 19

THE TRAGEDY OF RICHARD
THE THIRD

with the landing of Earl Richmond
and the Battle at Bosworth Field
by William Shakespeare
in the famous and popular
adaptation by the renowned
Colley Cibber

MR. JOHN BERRINGER TEMPLE as RICHARD III

The playbill continued with the cast of characters and
the actors listed on down below, but Steele stopped reading when he reached his own billing. His stage name was
now added to the long list of famous Richards: Cibber
himself, Garrick, Quin, Sheridan, Macklin, both Charles
and John Philip Kemble, Tree, Macready, Junius Brutus
Booth and, of course, the great Kean. He thought that he
could feel the blood racing through his veins as he went on
into the theater and made his way to the dressing room.
The lamp was lit in preparation for him. He turned it up.
The theater, even backstage, was almost deserted. He was
early. He stripped to his waist and sat down before the
mirror to apply his makeup. He had little to do other than
slightly to exaggerate his own features—dark eyebrows
which drew almost together in a sharp angle between his
eyes, a long aquiline nose, prominent high cheekbones,

finely sculptured full lips and a sharp chin. His black hair
he wore shoulder length, so he needed no wig for his role.
As he put the finishing touches on his makeup, darkening
his own thin black moustache and neatly trimmed goatee,
he sat back to admire his painting. He scowled. He smiled
a wry smile. He leered. He was pleased with the reflection
in the mirror.

"Ah," he said aloud to himself, "I shall be magnificent."

He washed the makeup off his hands, pulled off his boots
and trousers and went to the costume rack where he
dressed in the tights, boots and doublet of Richard, Duke
of Gloucester. One boot had a built-up heel inside to cause
him to walk with a limp. That had been his own idea, and
he was proud of it. A phony limp, he felt, was too easily
detected. With his built-up heel, he tried to walk straight,
and the resulting limp was genuine. The doublet was pad-
ded to display a slight hump on the back, and Steele tightened the muscles of his left arm to draw it up as if it were
withered. Again he studied himself in the mirror. Then he
tried a short speech to get the total effect:

> "Look how I am bewitch'd; behold mine
>   arm
> Is like a blasted sapling, wither'd up:
> And this is Edward's wife, that monstrous
>   witch,
> Consorted with that harlot strumpet
>   Shore,
> That by their witchcraft thus have marked
>   me."

Turning, he picked up a belt from which hung a jeweled
dagger, and buckled it around his waist. He was prepared.
He went to his greatcoat on the rack and withdrew a flask
from the pocket which he took to the dressing table. A
glass sat on the table. Steele poured it half full of rye

whiskey and drank it down. Then he poured it full and took a sip. He would relax until he was called.

Steele had emptied the glass three times when he heard a knock at his door.

"Mr. Temple," said a voice from outside the door, "you're wanted on stage."

"Thank you," said Steele. He stood up and walked to the door. Drawing up his left arm again and leering, he opened the door. He started for the stage, gliding with his limp. His movements were not those of a cripple. He was more like a spider. Mr. Hanley, the stage manager, met him at the entrance to the stage.

"We have a marvelous audience tonight, Mr. Temple," he said. "There's not an empty seat in the house."

"Wonderful," said Steele, and he crept out onto the stage. He turned around to survey the set. It was magnificently opulent—a fine background for his emergence as a brilliant star, he thought. He could see the other actors taking their places on the stage and in the wings—the one who would play King Edward, Clarence, the guards. It was almost time. Hanley came to him on the stage.

"Ready, Mr. Temple?"

Steele gave him a curt nod and moved to take his place. Hanley rushed off the stage. Steele stepped into the darkness of the wings to wait for the completion of the opening scene, the scene in the "Garden Within the Tower" added to the play by Colley Cibber in 1700 in which Stanley and Tressle describe to King Henry the Battle of Tewkesbury. At the end of the scene the curtain was drawn to respectful applause, during which Steele moved quickly to center stage. He took a deep breath and struck a careful pose. The curtain opened. Steele, his back to the audience, looked over his humped shoulder and glared at them. There was an audible gasp, a silence, then thunderous applause. The blood raced through Steele's veins. His heart pounded. As the applause began to fade, Steele slowly turned to face the audience, and he began his opening soliloquy.

> "Now is the winter of our discontent
> Made glorious summer by this sun of York;
> And all the clouds that loured upon our
> house
> In the deep bosom of the ocean buried.
> Now are our brows bound with victorious
> wreaths;
> Our bruised arms hung up for monuments;
> Our stern alarums changed to merry meet-
> ings,
> Our dreadful marches to delightful mea-
> sures."

The audience was spellbound, and Steele knew it. He had them. He could feel it. He was a success. He would be the next major star in the American theater. Now he knew it. He milked the speech for all it was worth, finishing with Richard's declared intention of mounting the throne of England with the first step up being upon the head of King Henry. Once more, the applause was thunderous. Steele moved forward and took his bows. The curtain closed for the changing of the scene, and Steele ran to take his place in the wings.

The second scene the adapter, Cibber, had pulled from another of Shakespeare's plays. The curtain opened to reveal the captured King Henry in the Tower. Steele slithered on stage.

"Good day, my lord," he said. "What, at your book so hard?"

Steele's very presence seemed to mesmerize the audience. They sat in rapt attention during the suspenseful exchange between Henry and Richard, tension building until Henry spoke his ill-fated lines:

"Teeth hadst thou in thy head when thou
      wast born,
To signify thou camest to bite the world:
And if the rest be true which I have heard,
Thou camest—"

Steele ripped out his sword and roared his interrupting
lines.

"I'll hear no more: die, prophet, in thy speech."

The depiction of the cold-blooded murder horrified the
audience, and at the same time, fascinated them. The actor playing Henry fell forward on his Bible, then rolled
over on his back displaying an abundance of stage blood.
And Steele as Richard stepped astride the body. He held
high his bloody sword.

"If any spark of life be yet remaining," he said in a cold,
unfeeling voice, "Down, down to hell; and say I sent thee
thither." He stabbed the body again and again. The stage
blood squirted from the prostrate body of the other actor,
and the audience gasped with horror. And the spell held.
Steele sustained the intensity through five acts of Shakespeare's long chronicle until his final line, "A horse! a
horse! my kingdom for a horse!" Actors playing Richmond
and his followers entered and hacked at Steele with their
stage blades bursting little packets of stage blood and finally "slitting his throat."

Back in his dressing room, Steele leaned back relaxing in
his chair, his legs stretched out in front of him, feet on the
edge of the dressing table. His feeling at the opening
speech had been correct. The play had been an overwhelming success. Steele had been called back again and
again by the ovations. The audience had stood up for him.
Even earlier, when at Bosworth Field, he had died,
snarling, hacked to death, he had heard the ladies scream,

and the stage manager had told him, after the final curtain, in between the praises and congratulations of fellow actors, fans and critics, that several ladies had actually fainted at his death scene. The evening had far exceeded his expectations, and his expectations had been grand indeed. He sat in the dressing room, savoring his success, dreaming of the future and relaxing after the long and strenuous role. He had pulled off the boots and had taken off the doublet. He had not yet removed his makeup, and he had a drink in his hand. There was a knock at the door.

"Who is it?" he shouted.

"Mr. Temple, may I come in please?"

It was a woman's voice. Steele threw a dressing gown over his shoulders and opened the door. A young lady, well dressed, no more than twenty years old, Steele judged, stood looking at him with unashamed admiration in her eyes.

"May I come in?"

"Please do."

The young lady swept into the room, closing the door behind her. Standing in the center of the floor, she turned to face Steele.

"Oh, Mr. Temple," she said, "you were marvelous. I've never seen anything before that thrilled me so. I almost fainted when you died. Oh, I hope you don't think me too bold."

"Not at all," said Steele. "I'm pleased that you enjoyed my performance."

"That is an understatement, Mr. Temple. I intend to return every night for the duration of the play. You, I believe, are the greatest actor ever to set foot on a stage in America—perhaps anywhere in the whole world. Of course, I've only seen theater in New York, but I've seen Booth and Forrest and even Irving when he came over from England, and you are so far above them all that it's pitiful to think of. I do so appreciate the privilege of watching you act."

She had moved closer to him, and Steele wondered what might be the young lady's intentions in coming to his dressing room like this—unescorted. He had lingered on the stage behind the closed curtain long enough, after the crowds had finally left him alone, to allow anyone who wished to have access to him the opportunity. Yet this one had waited, deliberately it would seem, until the crowds were gone and the actor had retired to his dressing room and was alone. She had also boldly entered his room, in spite of the fact that he was not fully dressed, and she, not he, had closed the door. Her intentions, he chuckled to himself, must be entirely dishonorable. He had heard that Booth and Forrest both had women flinging themselves upon them everywhere they went. Well, now it was to be his turn. It did not really fit the personality of Bluford Steele, but, he thought, it suited John Berringer Temple perfectly. It was right for this new image, this new identity, he had created. Bluford Steele was dead, he thought. Now long live J. B. Temple. What a long ways he had come. What a strange world it was.

He set his glass on the dressing table, carelessly allowing the dressing gown to slip off his shoulders and fall to the floor. He stepped to the young lady and put his hands on her shoulders. He looked into her eyes, his expression deliberately intense.

"I've been told before," he said, "that my talents were—well, shall we say—above average. But never before have I been given such a great compliment that meant so much to me. I shall never forget it."

"Oh, Mr. Temple."

The lady's eyelids fluttered. She trembled. Goose bumps covered her bare arms and shoulders.

"You are an extremely beautiful young woman."

She closed her eyes and tilted her head back.

"Oh, Mr. Temple."

Steele stared at her closed eyes, her arched neck, her slightly parted and inviting lips. She moved toward him with her bosom, and her bosom heaved with her deep, fast breaths. Steele pulled her gently toward him, and their lips met for a brief and tender kiss.

"Mr. Temple."

"You are lovely," he said.

Once again they kissed—this time longer and with more passion. Her arms slithered around Steele's waist. Steele pressed her to his bare chest as he felt her lips part and his passion grow. He wondered if he should ask her to meet him someplace—someplace more discreet. Perhaps he should offer to pick her up in a carriage at some place of her choice. Certainly the dressing room was not the spot to allow this sort of thing to continue, nor were his rooms a fitting place to entertain a young lady of social standing. Perhaps if he had time to prepare, they could be made respectable enough, but there would not be time for that this evening. No. He would have to hire a carriage and obtain a hotel room—a nice hotel room. How to register, he wondered. Under a false name? No, of course not. He was too well known in New York. He almost chuckled to himself. He was known, of course, under a false name already. How then? As man and wife? Probably not. It would be best, he decided, to register alone and then to slip the young lady up to the room later unnoticed. Yes. That would be the way. Their lips finally parted and Steele took a deep breath. The lady was panting.

"I don't know your name," he said.

She opened her lips to speak, but the next sound that Steele heard did not come from her mouth.

"Angelina!"

The name had been shouted by a great bulk of a man who, having suddenly flung open the door to the dressing room, stood filling the space where it had been. The lady stepped quickly away from Steele and screamed. Steele jumped back from her.

"What is the meaning of this?" he shouted indignantly. "This is a private dressing room."

The bulk stood in the doorway, his chest heaving with righteous anger. His eyes were wide and flashing as he took in the scene.

"So," he said, looking at the girl, "this is the way you congratulate Mr. Temple, is it?"

"Chester," she said.

"Sir," said Steele, "I don't know you, and I have only just met the young lady. If you will allow me—"

"Bah," roared Chester. " 'Chester dear,' she says, 'wait for me outside the theater,' she says. 'I know you must be bored with all this,' she says, 'so just be a dear and bring round the carriage for me,' she says. 'I'll just be a minute to congratulate Mr. Temple,' she says. A minute, indeed. Congratulate, indeed. Mr. Temple, indeed."

"Sir," said Steele, "I'm afraid you've gotten the wrong impression. The young lady's behavior was entirely above reproach."

While he was talking, Steele awkwardly reached for his dressing gown which still lay on the floor where he had earlier let it fall. While he was bent over reaching for the gown, Chester raised his knurly walking stick and made for Steele.

"I'll congratulate you, Mr. Temple," he shouted. "Mr. Actor. Mr. King Richard, you."

He swung the knurly stick with all his might, the blow landing with a terrible force across Steele's bare shoulders, knocking him off balance and leaving a long red mark on Steele's skin. Before Steele could recover, a second blow caught him on the buttocks, causing him to stumble forward. Steele yelped and groped for the top of the dressing table for something to grab onto to help him pull himself to his feet. Quite by accident, his right hand found the jeweled knife of King Richard where he had tossed it on the table earlier. A third blow caught him low across the back. He screamed and flinched, and visions of past violence swirled in his head. He forgot where he was—who Chester was. He forgot the role of John B. Temple and was again Blue Steele, wronged and tormented. He drew the knife and whirled.

"Dog," he said, and he drove the blade into Chester's belly.

As Chester grabbed for his middle trying desperately to stanch the flow of blood that gushed from the hole Steele had poked in him, the color fading from his face, his eyes opened wide in astonished horror, his knees slowly buckling, the girl began to scream again. Steele had been staring in disbelief at what he had done, but the hysterical shrieking of this woman, on whom he had so recently been plotting, brought him somewhat back to his senses.

"Be quiet," he hissed.

She continued to scream, her gaze transfixed on Chester.

"Shut up."

The shrieks did not subside, and Steele wondered how he could have been so enamored of such a mindless bauble. Suddenly she disgusted him. She also, he realized, was endangering him. Her screams would certainly bring someone soon to investigate. He thought about hitting her on the jaw to knock her out, or at least to shut her up. He drew back his fist, but he couldn't quite bring himself to do it. In desperation he grabbed her and clamped a hand over her screaming mouth, and suddenly she swooned, slumping back into the chair at the dressing table. Steele was greatly relieved, but he had no idea how long a swoon would incapacitate a woman. Chester had fallen to the floor in a pool of his own blood and had ceased his gurgling breaths. He was apparently dead. Steele raced to the door and looked out. No one was in sight, but someone must have heard, he thought. The screams were too many and too loud to have gone unnoticed. He shut the door and locked it, then stood for a moment staring at the jeweled dagger in his hand, its blade dripping blood. Then he realized what had caused Angelina to faint. When he had grabbed her to shut her up, the dagger had been in his hand. She must have thought that he was planning to kill her too.

"Oh, I am fortune's fool," he wailed, and he tossed the dagger away. "I must get out of here quickly."

He began dressing hurriedly and was just buttoning his vest when he heard a knock at the door. He felt his heart skip a beat.

"Yes," he shouted, a bit too loudly and quickly, he thought.

"Mr. Temple?"

He recognized the voice of Hanley, the stage manager, but he did not immediately reply, and the voice came again, the second time with a bit more urgency.

"Mr. Temple."

"Yes. What is it?"

"We heard someone screaming."

"Well, check with the women," shouted Steele. "It certainly wasn't me. I heard it myself, and it sounded awful. You'd better get to the bottom of it right away."

"Yes sir. Thank you, sir."

Steele realized that he was still wearing his stage makeup, and he deliberately slowed himself down. He took the makeup off his face. He must, he decided, be calm. He must figure out what's best to do. He finished dressing. He couldn't hide the body. Besides, the woman was a witness. He couldn't bring himself to deliberately murder her in order to cover his trail, and he knew that he couldn't defend himself for the killing of Chester by calling it self-defense, although, of course, it really was. Chester was undoubtedly the woman's husband, and any jury

would believe that Chester had had every right to beat
Steele silly with his damnable stick, even kill him, under
the circumstances, and that Steele had had no right to
defend himself—particularly with a knife against a stick.
Damned Philistines, he thought. No. There was no way
out of this mess, and the woman might come to her senses
at any time. He didn't really want to have to deal with
that. He was finished. His brilliant career had begun and
come to an end all in one evening. He was a murderer, and
soon all of New York would know. He had to get away, but
how? And where would he go?

He fastened his cloak around his neck and poured himself another glass of rye whiskey. He tossed down the
drink, put the flask in his greatcoat pocket and took a last
look around the dressing room—the star's dressing room
in Booth's Theater in New York City. He looked at the lady
slumped in the chair. There was Chester in a pool of his
own blood with the pale and ghastly expression of death
on his face, and there on the floor, the bloody jeweled
dagger. His eye fell on Chester's knurly walking stick, and
for some reason, he picked it up. Then he closed the little
wooden box that contained his personal makeup, left the
dressing room and the theater and began walking the dark
streets of the city.

Sometime during the evening a thick fog had rolled in
and blanketed the city. It made Steele feel comfortable at
first. It helped to hide him. Then it reminded him of home
—the wooded hills and valleys of the western Cherokee
Nation bordering Arkansas Territory, the place his family
and hundreds of other Cherokee families had made home
after the United States government had forced them to
leave their ancestral lands in the East which had become
the states of Georgia, Alabama, Tennessee, North and
South Carolina. Steele had no memory of Cherokee life in
the East, but he had heard his parents and his grandpar-

ents speak of it as if they had been speaking of a deceased ancestor. That eastern land was their lost homeland. His was the western Cherokee Nation. He had come a long ways, he thought, a young Cherokee expatriate with no home, no family. He had created a new identity, found a new home in the theater, a new life. He had worked hard and had climbed to the top, and now he had thrown it all away. He was back where he had started—an exile with no home and no name. The fog reminded him of something warm and comfortable in his first lost life. The fog reminded him of home.

CHAPTER TWO

Bluford Steele was thirty years old the night he made his appearance as John Berringer Temple playing King Richard III at Booth's Theater on Twenty-third Street between Fifth and Sixth avenues in New York City. He had been in 1843 in a small community called Gideon in the Cherokee Nation in what was destined to later become the northeastern portion of the state of Oklahoma. His father, Chickenhawk, known to the *yonegs*, or whites, as Frank Steele, was a full-blood Cherokee who had joined with Major Ridge and others known as the Treaty Party in the days before the long walk known as the Trail of Tears. The Treaty Party was made up of Cherokees, largely but not entirely mixed-bloods, who had begun to believe that removal from their homelands to the new lands in the West was inevitable. They did not believe that it was right, but they felt that the United States government under the administration of Old Hickory, Andrew Jackson, was determined to move the Cherokees, and that the longer the Cherokees resisted, the harder the eventual move would be on them. So they had signed a removal treaty in the name of their entire nation, knowing that the more conservative members of their tribe, including their legitimately elected tribal government, would believe them to be traitors. They knew well the Cherokee law that called for the death of any Cherokee found guilty of selling or trading away tribal lands. Yet they believed that signing the treaty was in the best interests of the Cherokee people, and so they signed. Major Ridge had signed his name

to the infamous document, stepped back and sighed a
deep sigh.

"I feel that I have just signed my death warrant," he
said.

Major Ridge's statement proved to be prophetic. The
Treaty Party members had moved to the West voluntarily
after having signed the treaty. The majority of Cherokees,
known as the Ross Party for their leader, Principal Chief
John Ross, had remained behind and resisted removal until the United States Army had been sent to round them up
and forcibly march them to the land in the West. Many had
died along the way. It was said that not one Cherokee
family escaped the tragedy of the Trail of Tears. Those
who suffered the march were bitter, not only against the
United States, but also against the Treaty Party, the members of which they did indeed see as traitors. They invoked
the ancient law against the selling of tribal land, and they
began to assassinate the men who were guilty of having
signed the treaty. Major Ridge had been shot from ambush. His son, John, was stabbed to death. Elias Boudinot
was hacked to death in front of his own house with an ax.

Bluford Steele remembered through the fog of New
York City the morning when long before John B. Temple
existed or had ever been thought of, in another life in a
time in which he had been known as Bluford Steele, the
son of Chickenhawk, his father had gone out early as usual
to tend to chores around the house. Twelve men had rid-
den up on horseback. He, the child called Blue, had been
behind the house. He had come round the house in time to
see twelve men shoot from horseback. He had seen his
father jerk and fall—had seen his body lying on the ground
covered with blood and twitching with each additional
shot fired into it. He had heard his mother scream, had
seen the men ride off, had watched his mother run to the
body no longer recognizable to him as his father and

gather the bloody mess into her arms, and he remembered it all vividly in the fog on the sidewalks of New York City.

Steele thought of his mother, the daughter of northern missionaries who had gone to Georgia to work among the Cherokee Indians. She had been gently raised by her parents and properly educated. She loved good music and literature and took delight in long after-dinner conversations with cultured folks. Yet she had fallen in love with Chickenhawk and married him, and Chickenhawk had become what they called "a progressive." Though he had been brought up in the fashion of a traditional Cherokee, he had enrolled their son in school. After the death of Chickenhawk, Bluford Steele's mother had moved with her child to Springfield, Missouri, to escape the violence of the Cherokee Nation, and when he was old enough, she had sent him north to college.

He remembered stepping off the train in Hanover, New Hampshire. He had been overwhelmed by the buildings, the noise and the crowds of people. He had stood dumbfounded, confused. He had felt an overwhelming urge to turn around and get back on the train, but he had realized that it was headed in the wrong direction to take him back home again. He had wondered if it would somehow turn around and go back. Then he felt a hand on his shoulder and he jumped. He looked around, trying to compose himself, and found himself looking at the chest of a ponderous man in a black suit with a gold watch chain stretched across the black vest which barely buttoned around his girth.

"And is this young Mr. Steele from Missouri?" boomed the big man's voice.

Blue looked up into the face that went with the black mass before him. It was kindly enough, though somehow arrogant at the same time. It had a benign smile upon it and a twinkle in its faded blue eyes. Its hair, slightly unruly under a black, flat-brimmed hat, was white.

"Uh, yes," stammered Blue. "Yes sir. I'm Bluford Steele."

He shifted his small grip from his right to his left hand and offered his right which the portly gentleman squeezed as if he would crunch it.

"Reverend Jeremiah Wiget, my boy," he roared. "Your Grandfather Bentley was a dear friend of mine—a dear friend of many years. I must say, you don't favor him at all."

"No sir," said Blue. "They tell me that I favor my father."

"Yes, I dare say. The savage features do show through a bit. Well, come along, my lad. You've had a long journey. You must get cleaned up and rested. Tomorrow I'll introduce you to the college."

The drive in Reverend Wiget's carriage from the depot through the streets of Hanover to the Reverend's house was for Blue Steele a trip through a strange and wonderful land.

"Close your mouth, my boy," roared the Reverend with a laugh. "You may swallow a bug."

Eventually the carriage drew up before a large, white house—a mansion, thought Blue—and a black man in a tie and tails opened the door.

"Take the young man's bags, Charles," puffed the Reverend, as he climbed out of the carriage.

"Yes sir, Reverend," said Charles, reaching for the bag. Blue allowed Charles to take the grip from him.

"Thank you," he said, still staring at the large, white house.

Charles rushed ahead of Blue and the Reverend to open the front door of the mansion. Inside the Reverend led Blue to the parlor.

"Ladies," he roared, "young Mr. Steele."

A dowdy, gray-haired lady stood up, laid aside her tatting and offered a limp hand to Blue.

"Welcome, Mr. Steele," she said. "I'm Mrs. Wiget, and this is our daughter, Grace."

Blue took the lady's hand.

"How do you do, ma'am," he said. Then he turned toward Grace.

"Hello, Mr. Steele," said the girl, and her bright eyes sparkled beneath long lashes. She looked and sounded to Blue Steele like a thousand angels, and when her hand touched his, he felt his knees tremble, and he couldn't make his voice work. He was jolted back to earth by the booming voice of the Reverend.

"Charles, show Mr. Steele to his room and draw his bath for him."

"Yes sir."

"Mr. Steele, follow Charles. He'll see to your needs. We'll have supper at seven."

Sitting in his bath, Blue tried to recall every feature of Grace Wiget.

"I've never seen such a beautiful girl," he said to himself.

Napping after his bath, he dreamed of her, and though he was careful not to show it, he was greatly aggravated when Charles woke him from the sweet dream to dress for supper.

Supper was difficult for Blue. He was ravenously hungry because of his long journey, but he was distracted by the charms of Grace, and the Reverend with great mouthfuls of food insisted on badgering him with questions. He asked about Grandfather Silas, about his mother, about his previous schooling, about church services in Missouri, about Blue's hopes for the future and about the rail trip from Springfield to Hanover. Blue had been trained since childhood to eat quietly and never to talk with food in his mouth. He found it to be nearly impossible to eat without rudely ignoring the Reverend's barrage of inquiries.

At long last the supper was finished, and while Charles cleared the table, the family, with Blue in tow, adjourned to the parlor for polite conversation and some piano music from Grace. Blue was fascinated by Grace's playing, and he was disappointed when the Reverend called an end to the evening and sent everyone off to bed.

Blue soon grew used to Hanover and to Hanoverians. He adapted well at Dartmouth and became, if not an outstanding student, at least a good one. He was the pride of the Dartmouth faculty, a young Indian from the wilds who was developing a fine gentlemanly polish and progressing beyond their expectations in his education. His Greek and Latin were both fair, and his skill at composition in English was quite good. He had an excellent facility for memorization. But mainly, he was a gentleman in all respects.

"Of course," the good Reverend Wiget was heard to remark occasionally, "the boy is really only half Indian. His mother comes from an excellent old Boston family. Her father, the Reverend Silas Bentley, rest his soul, was a dear and longtime friend of mine."

For the next two years Blue's education progressed and his ties to the Wiget family increased. He felt obligated to the Reverend and to Mrs. Wiget. They had taken him in. They saw to his needs. They provided for his education. They did not, somehow, seem close to him, even after two years. They were stiff and formal. They were kind, yet they maintained a distance. Blue felt that, somehow, for the Wigets, he was a showpiece, an object of pride and satisfaction, but not of real affection. But with Grace it was different. He spent long hours with Grace. He felt good just being in her presence, and as time went by, his admiration for her charm and beauty grew into a deep affection and a passion. Blue felt that he was in love. What was more, though he did not dare to believe it, he felt that she was returning his affection. She seemed to enjoy the time they spent alone in the parlor or in the yard just talking. She could not get enough, it seemed to Blue, of his tales of his past. She longed to hear him tell of the culture and the traditions of the Cherokee people, and though it always made her cry, she begged again and again to hear the tales of the Trail of Tears and its aftermath—the tragic civil war among the Cherokees that had cost the life of Chickenhawk. The two years passed quickly.

Then came the night that Brice Seagraves' traveling theatrical company stopped over on tour at Hanover with *Othello,* the great Seagraves himself, of course, appearing in the title role. Blue attended the play with the Wigets, and following the performance, Reverend Wiget had a gathering of clergy and of Dartmouth faculty over for discussion and refreshments.

"I had always taken Othello's tragic flaw to be the passion of jealousy," said Reverend Twitty, following a gulp of sherry, "but Mr. Seagraves' interpretation of the role has given me quite a different impression."

"Mr. Seagraves was magnificent," roared Reverend Wiget.

"Yes, of course he was," said Professor Barnstorm, "but Reverend Twitty's remark has twitted, if you'll pardon the pun, my curiosity. Othello is certainly a jealous man."

"Oh," said Reverend Twitty, "I don't deny his jealousy, but there is something else, perhaps more profound, at the bottom of it."

Blue Steele had been engrossed in studying the features of Grace who was seated across the room from him, but the conversation regarding Seagraves' interpretation of Othello captured at least a part of his attention.

"And what is this profound something?" sneered Professor Barnstorm.

"For all his seeming education and high position in a

highly civilized city," said Reverend Twitty, "Othello seems, and Mr. Seagraves' interpretation, I believe, supports this idea, Othello seems to have retained at the base of his character a certain savagery. He is a raging beast inside, though somewhat refined on the outside."

Blue Steele furrowed his brow as Reverend Twitty continued.

"The basic problem of the play, then, is not Othello's jealousy. If that were the case, he may as well have been a civilized Venetian. The basic problem, I submit, is that Othello is a savage in the midst of civilization."

"An interesting theory," blurted out Reverend Wiget.

"Hmm," hummed Professor Barnstorm, stroking his chin.

"An interesting theory, yes," said Blue Steele, suddenly interjecting himself into the discussion, "but one which, I'm afraid, if taken seriously, would raise questions about the futility of Dartmouth College in undertaking the education of such an individual as myself."

"Why, whatever do you mean, my boy?" said Reverend Wiget.

"Am I, too," said Blue, "a raging beast covered with the mere outward trappings of civilization? I think not, but I would offer another interpretation of the play."

"Remember your place, Blue," said Reverend Wiget, "and don't be presumptuous with my distinguished guests."

"No, no, Jeremiah," said Professor Barnstorm, "let's hear what the lad has to say."

"I believe that the problem with Mr. Seagraves' interpretation lies with his makeup," said Blue.

"Oh, come now," said Wiget.

"Makeup?" said Barnstorm. "How?"

"Why, Mr. Seagraves was practically white," said Blue, "yet the play makes it perfectly clear that Othello was a black man."

"Black? He couldn't be black," roared Wiget.

"But he himself refers to himself as black, sir," said Blue. " 'Haply for I am black,' he says. Brabantio describes him with a 'sooty bosom,' and Roderigo calls him 'the thick lips.' I believe that it's clear from the text that Othello is a black African."

"Shakespeare," said Reverend Twitty, "would never have committed such an indiscretion as to couple the fair Desdemona with a Negro."

"But the text . . ." began Blue.

"But what has all this to do with the argument?" said Barnstorm. "Even if we were to grant you your point, which we will not, what has that to do with the flaw of jealousy in his character or with the idea of basic savagery which Reverend Twitty has propounded?"

"Sir," said Blue, "I think that I am in a position to empathize with the predicament in which Othello found himself. I am an American Indian. I am brown-skinned. And I find myself in a world of white people. The people of Hanover have been good to me and I love them, but I need no more reminder than a glance at the skin on the back of my hands that I am alone. I am different. I'm an Indian in a white man's world, and I'm constantly aware of that often painful fact. Othello was a black man in a world of white men. He was therefore, I believe, more vulnerable to the evil insinuations of Iago. He felt insecure. His position in society was, at best, tenuous. By avoiding the black makeup, Mr. Seagraves misleads his audience. He robs us of an essential element of Othello's nature—his race—his differentness in the society of Venice."

"Bosh," said Reverend Wiget.

"Perhaps the lad has something there," mused Professor Barnstorm.

"Shakespeare would never have coupled a Negro to a white woman," said Reverend Twitty.

"I think, perhaps, I should excuse myself," said Blue. "I apologize if I've offended anyone."

"Good night," said Reverend Wiget.

Blue glanced at Grace as he turned to leave the room, and he noticed a blush on her face. He bade the company good night and climbed the stairs to his room. He took off his jacket, tie and shoes and sat down in the dark to relax. After a while, he did not know how long, he heard a faint tapping at his door. Blue opened the door, and Grace rushed inside, closing it behind her.

"Grace," said Blue.

"Shhh."

She put her hand over his mouth, and the touch of her sent a thrill throughout his body. He felt as if he were being touched by an angel.

"I had to see you," she said. "Father was unfair. What you said about the play was perceptive. It was very bright, and they should have listened to you with courtesy, at least."

"Thank you," said Blue. "I don't value their opinions in the least, but yours means everything to me."

Grace threw her arms around Blue's neck and pulled his face to hers. She kissed him full on the mouth. Then, while he was still overwhelmed, too astonished and overcome to react, she rushed back to the door and opened it.

"I love you," she said, and she flashed into the hall, closing the door behind her.

With the next day's post Blue Steele received the news of his mother's death in Springfield, Missouri. He was alone. A Cherokee belongs to his mother's clan, and since Blue's mother was a white woman, he had no clan. He had no Cherokee relatives. He was not even, according to a strictly traditional point of view, a Cherokee, but he did not feel like a white man. He wondered if he should consider his home to be in Hanover with the Wigets. Grace had said, "I love you." He sat in the dark on the edge of his bed. The letter had fallen to the floor. He took a deep breath, and as he let it out, he let his head fall backward so that he stared up at the ceiling, and he recited aloud, but in a low voice, some lines from *Othello*.

> "She loved me for the dangers I had
>   passed,
> And I loved her that she did pity them."

Reverend Wiget leaned back from the supper table, and holding his linen napkin up to his lips, belched deeply.

"Excuse me," he said, "but that feels much better out than in."

Mrs. Wiget and Grace got up from their chairs, excused themselves and left the room. Charles began clearing the table.

"Reverend," said Blue, "I'd like to speak to you privately, if I may."

"Privately is it?" said Wiget.

"Yes sir. If I may."

"Well then, we'll go into the parlor and talk while I have my after-supper cigar. Come along, my boy."

Reverend Wiget, placing his hands on the arms of his chair, heaved himself puffing up and out of the chair.

"Yes sir," said Blue, rising to follow the Reverend out of the dining room and into the parlor. Reverend Wiget opened a cigar box on top of a sideboard and removed a cigar. He snipped the end of it, laid down the scissors and began to roll the cigar around in his mouth to moisten it.

"Well, what is it, lad?" he said, striking a match on the sideboard.

"Sir," said Blue, "I believe that I'm progressing well in my studies."

"Quite well indeed," puffed Reverend Wiget.

"And I should be able soon to obtain a position as a

schoolteacher and to earn a decent living at it, don't you think?"

"I should say that you're already more than qualified for such a position, especially on the frontier."

"And with such a position, I should be able easily to support a wife and family."

"Ha, ha, ha," chuckled the Reverend. "Plenty of time for that, my boy. Plenty of time."

"But I could?"

"Yes. Yes, indeed you could."

"Then, sir," said Blue, "I should like to ask you a question."

"There's no need for hesitation," said the Reverend, a benign smile on his face. "Think of me as a father. I want you to feel that you can always come to me, my boy."

"I would like very much to think of you as a father, sir," said Blue. "Sir, I'm in love with Grace. I want to marry her. I'd like your permission to ask your daughter for her hand."

Reverend Wiget could not respond at first. His eyes opened wide. He slowly turned his back on Blue and stood silently puffing his cigar. Blue began to wring his hands. He wondered if the Reverend would ever answer his question. Finally Wiget spoke.

"No."

"But, sir . . ." Blue began.

"Young man," said the Reverend, turning to again face Blue, "to begin with, my daughter is not ready to marry. She is too young. I'm not prepared to give up my child yet."

"She's old enough to marry," said Blue. "And she loves me."

"Has she said so much?"

"Yes, she has."

"Do you mean to tell me that under my own roof, while

I've been treating you as a son, you've been sneaking around making love to my daughter?"

"We've spoken . . ."

"You ingrate."

"Sir, we've done nothing wrong. Nothing improper."

"It's highly improper for a red-skinned savage to make love to a decent white girl."

"Savage?"

The Reverend stammered. He put a hand to his brow. "Forgive me, Blue," he said. "Forgive me. I spoke in haste and anger. I . . . The truth is . . . What I meant to say, or rather, should have said, is that a marriage between one of your background and culture and a child like Grace could never work. You're from the wilds of the Indian Territory. She's never been more than sixty miles from Hanover. No. No, it's impossible."

"It's true that I was born in the Cherokee Nation," said Blue, "but from early childhood I've been raised by my mother, a white woman and a missionary's daughter, in the church and in her schools in Springfield, Missouri. My background is not so different from that of Grace."

"I'm trying to be reasonable with you."

"By calling me names?"

"I apologized for that and now there's an end to it. I'll hear no more. You'll not have my permission to marry my daughter. Not now—not ever. We'll have to find you other lodgings. I'll not send you back to Missouri and deprive you of further education. I'll not do that. I'll locate other lodgings for you here in Hanover. I'll do that first thing tomorrow."

Alone in his room, Blue wondered if the good Reverend felt safe with a savage under his roof.

"Brabantio," he said.

He tried to read, but he could not. He kept envisioning the features of the beautiful Grace. He recalled the angry words—the insulting words—of Reverend Wiget. He saw

the puffed and reddened face, and he was alternately
ashamed, enraged and stricken with grief and longing. He
felt that he could not bear the pain much more.

Grace tugged on the rope ends tied to her bed. Satisfied
that they were tight enough, she moved to the open window and tossed out an armload of rope which unraveled
on its way down to become a ladder. From a shadow at the
back of the yard, Blue Steele emerged and ran to the foot
of the ladder. Grace dropped a small suitcase out the window for Blue to catch. Then she climbed out and began
her descent. Blue's heart was pounding in his chest. As
soon as Grace's feet touched the ground, Blue drew her to
him and held her close.

"Blue," said Grace, "we must hurry away from here
before I'm missed."

"Come on," said Blue, taking her by the hand and picking up her suitcase in the other.

They ran hard heading for the street where Blue had a
hired carriage waiting, but as they rounded the corner of
the house, Blue ran smack into the massive frame of Reverend Wiget. Grace screamed.

"Daddy."

Blue staggered back a few steps. He looked up at Rever-
end Wiget who glared at him with a fierceness to which
Blue was unaccustomed. Standing on either side of the
Reverend were Mr. Gill and Mr. Dillon, members of the
Reverend's congregation. Wiget stepped forward raising
his fat right hand above his head.

"Judas," he roared, and he slapped Blue hard across the
face flinging him to one side and to the ground.

"Daddy, stop," said Grace. "I love him."

"Hold your tongue," said the Reverend, and he grabbed
his daughter by the arm. Without another word, he
dragged her to the front door and into the house. Blue

heard the door slam. He raised himself up on one elbow, but Gill delivered him a hard and swift kick in the ribs.

"Thought he could get himself a white girl," said Gill.

"Preacher's daughter to boot," said Dillon, adding his kick to that of Gill.

Gill dragged Blue to his feet, and Dillon drove a fist into Blue's stomach. Blue felt sick. He wanted to pass out, to fall down, but Gill kept holding him up. Dillon hit him again in the belly, then, taking him by the hair, lifted his face up to make a target of it. His punch loosened one or two teeth in Blue's mouth and brought a stream of crimson trickling down his chin. Then Gill once again threw Blue to the ground. Blue was on his face in the yard. He dragged his knees up under his belly, fighting the pain, trying to clear his head. Gill and Dillon stepped up close, one on each side of Blue. Almost in unison, they unfastened their belt buckles and pulled their belts off from around their waists. As Blue pushed himself up to his hands and knees, Gill lashed him across the back with his belt. Blue felt the sharp pain course through his body. Before he realized what he was doing, he screamed, but the scream was no sooner out of his lungs than Dillon's belt came slicing through the night air. Blue collapsed onto the ground again. His fingers clutched the close-cut grass of Reverend Wiget's yard as Dillon and Gill alternately beat him with their belts.

"Hold it," said Gill. "That's enough." And the beating stopped. "Now, boy, you get out of here."

Blue groaned and tried to get up. Dillon lashed him again across the back.

"He said move, redskin."

Blue struggled again to his hands and knees only to receive a kick in the seat from Gill which drove him back to the ground.

"Get going," said Gill, "and don't stop until you're back in your wigwam."

"You hang around here until daylight," said Dillon, "looking for more white girls, we'll finish you."

Blue finally struggled to his feet and staggered to the edge of the yard. He could hear the taunts and threats of Gill and Dillon behind him as he left the yard and stumbled into the street. The coach he had hired was gone. He made his way on foot painfully down the road until he felt that he was a safe distance from the Reverend's house, then he collapsed in a roadside ditch and slowly drifted into oblivion. Out of the darkness Grace came toward him wearing a beautiful white gown that swirled behind her in the wind. Her long, blond curls bounced on her shoulders, and she smiled a happy, girlish smile. Blue reached out to clutch her in his arms, but as he did, she faded away, and in her place, the massive form of Reverend Wiget appeared.

"Savage," it roared. "Heathen."

"I am not," shouted Blue.

"Stay away from my daughter."

"She loves me."

"Then she is abused, stolen from me, and corrupted
By spells and medicines bought of mountebanks;
For Nature so preposterously to err,
Being not deficient, blind, or lame of sense,
Sans witchcraft could not."

The Reverend then began to slap Blue, first with one hand, then the other, but Blue stood his ground until great broganned feet began to tromp him. He saw the feet stamping at him. He saw the faces of Reverend Wiget and of Dillon and Gill. Wiget snarled and cursed. Dillon and Gill laughed and jeered.

"Savage."

"Indian."

"I'm not."

Blue sat up with a start. He was perspiring heavily. He did not at first know where he was, but he felt the pain. He looked around him. It was dark and he was alone.

Blue Steele waited in the loft of the big barn on the Gill farm at the edge of Hanover. He waited with a rope he had fashioned into a lariat of sorts. Now and then from his perch he could see Mrs. Gill come out of the house on some errand or other and then go back in. Finally, Gill came in from the fields. He went into the house, Blue thought it must be for supper. It was nearly dark before he came back out and headed for the barn. Blue became conscious that his lips were very dry. Gill pushed open the big door and stepped into the darkness of the barn. Knowing the layout by heart, he strode confidently to a lantern which hung on a peg below the loft and lit it. As he replaced the globe, he felt something slap him about the shoulders, but before he could react, it tightened around his neck. He grabbed for it and found that it was a noose and that it was being pulled from up above him. He tried to scream, but already the noose was too tight. He could only gag. He felt himself being drawn upward, and he thought that he was going to be strangled to death, but when the tips of his toes could still barely scratch the barn floor, the pulling stopped. The rope remained tight. He was left to push with his toes, to try to keep his weight on his toes rather than on the rope around his neck. He was left scratching, spinning and gagging. Someone would find him and cut him down eventually. He would not die, but he would never forget how close he had come to death.

Blue Steele left Hanover, but not before Dillon's Hardware Store had been burned to the ground. He left Hanover feeling that he was a lost soul, a man with no home, no place to go, no real identity. He was surprised that, once that feeling had set in, he did not really feel that the loss of Grace had been so terrible. Grace was simply a part of the whole lost life which was behind him. But it didn't take him long to decide where to go. He needed a new life, a new identity. He thought of Brice Seagraves and his theatrical company. He liked reading Shakespeare, and he had enjoyed watching the performance. He imagined that he could act. He knew that he would enjoy playing Shakespeare. Seagraves was from New York City, and it was to New York City and the Seagraves Company that Blue Steele went.

Seagraves, of course, did not know Blue Steele. Blue had only been one member of the audience to which Seagraves had played Othello in Hanover. Blue didn't tell the actor that he had seen him in Hanover. He simply told him that he wanted to act and that he was willing to work in any capacity necessary with the company in order to learn the craft. Seagraves had been immediately taken by the young man's "dark, Mediterranean look." (Blue did not tell him that he was Indian.) In short, he had been hired, and he had given a false name. John Berringer Temple was created, and Temple's career had been dazzling. He learned fast. He was soon acting in major roles for Seagraves, and it wasn't long before he had outgrown the small touring company. He was beginning to be known widely in theatrical circles, and at long last, he had received an offer to play the title role in Shakespeare's *The Tragedy of Richard the Third* at Booth's Theater in New York City.

CHAPTER THREE

Steele wandered aimlessly through the foggy streets of New York City, his mind recalling episodes from a former life. He remembered the discussion in Reverend Wiget's parlor regarding basic savagery which he had so resented at the time, and then he thought of Gill choking and gagging at the end of a rope in his own barn, of Dillon's store and, finally, of Chester in the dressing room. *Perhaps they were right,* he thought. *Perhaps I am a savage at heart.* He thought of Othello and Desdemona, of Blue Steele and Grace, and of John B. Temple and—what was her name? Angelina. He thought of the apparently recurring pattern of his life—or lives. The young Blue Steele, an Indian child driven from his home in the Cherokee Nation by violence, the young Dartmouth scholar with high hopes, the promise thrown away by acts of violence, and the fast-rising star J. B. Temple, his ascent halted for the same reason. He wondered if he were doomed to be a man without an identity, constantly beginning again. A passing carriage startled him out of his reverie. He jumped into an alleyway and waited for the sounds of the carriage to fade away into the depths of the soothing fog. Then he thought again of Brice Seagraves.

Steele used the knurly walking stick to pound on the door of the room that he knew had been the temporary residence of Brice Seagraves. Seagraves and Company, he knew, were due to leave New York on a western tour the very next day. No, Steele thought, today, this very morning. He cursed himself for not having thought of Seagraves sooner. He had wandered dark streets for most of the night, and now it would soon be daylight. What if Seagraves and Company had already left the city? Steele rapped again on the door with the heavy, knobbed stick. Then he heard a voice from inside the room.

"Knock, knock, knock. Who's there, i' th' name of Belzebub? Knock, knock. Who's there in th' other devil's name?"

"Thank God," said Steele. "Brice," he shouted, "open up quickly."

The door opened enough for Brice Seagraves to peek out and see who it was had disturbed his rest so early in the morning.

"Brice, for God's sake, let me in, man."

Steele didn't wait for a reply but shoved his way past Seagraves and into the room where he dropped unceremoniously into an overstuffed chair.

"Temple?" said Seagraves. "Temple, what the hell are you doing out and about at this time of the night? By God, sir, I saw your opening-night performance, and you were awesome as Richard Humpback. Simply awesome. But what's wrong with you, Johnny? What are you doing here?"

"You didn't see the entire performance, old fellow," said Steele. "I was attacked in my dressing room late last night, and I stabbed a man to death."

"What? Good heavens, man. But surely everything's resolved satisfactorily with the police. After all, if you were attacked in your own dressing room—why, that's as if you'd been attacked in your own home."

"Ordinarily, yes," replied Steele, "but in this case, the man's wife was there first, and he found her in a rather compromising situation and myself, alas, somewhat *déshabillé*."

"Oh, my."

"Yes, my friend. I'm afraid that I am a murderer. I killed the swine with Dickie's dagger."

Old Seagraves sank into a chair across from Steele. His expression was one of genuine concern. He had a fatherly feeling toward this fine young actor, and he felt as if he had a stake in the young star's career. He had taken him in as a youth and brought him along in the theater. He had helped establish the meteoric rise. He felt both love and admiration for this man who now slumped in his room, desperate and dejected.

"But what will you do, Johnny?" he said.

"That's why I've come to you, Brice. I need your help. I have to get away. To fly. You're leaving for the West. I could hide myself in the midst of your company long enough to get well away from New York, then, well, who knows?"

"Johnny," said Seagraves, his old eyes lighting up, "I've just recently lost an actor. I could use you to play Macduff."

"Brice, I can't appear in public. They'll be looking for me. I'm a well-known actor."

"But they'll be looking for the famous star, John Berringer Temple. They wouldn't be looking for J. B. Temple in an obscure traveling company in the role of Macduff. And my whole company is new since you left us, Johnny. No one knows you. We'll call you, uh, Tyrone Hamlin. That's a good name for an aspiring young actor. What do you say, Tyrone?"

"Well, I . . ."

"Come, let's cut your hair and shave your face. Then we'll get you a change of clothes, and when the company gathers to be on our way, I'll introduce you as Tyrone Hamlin, an old friend from my days in the San Francisco theater and the newest addition to the company. Everyone will be relieved that our vacancy has been filled, and no one will suspect a thing."

"Another beginning," said Steele.

"What?"

"Nothing, Brice. Nothing at all."

The wagons containing actors, actresses, costumes, scenery and stage props moved West, and with them was a new actor called Tyrone Hamlin. He played Macduff in *Macbeth*. He played Mercutio in *Romeo and Juliet*. He proved to be a popular new actor with the company members as well as with the western audiences. He played his roles well, but he showed no ambition to take over the larger roles, no jealousy toward the stars. He was quiet and kept much to himself. But one day in St. Joseph, Missouri, he witnessed a gunfight. It wasn't his first glimpse of violence. As the young Blue Steele, he had seen plenty, and he had ruined his second life as John Berringer Temple by stabbing Chester. But this was different. He was sitting in a saloon having a drink of rye whiskey, which he had developed a taste for as J. B. Temple, when he heard a commotion in the street. Everyone in the saloon jumped up and ran for the door or for the windows in order to get a view into the street. Steele followed to see what it was all about. Out in the middle of the street was a man with a six-gun in his right hand. He was yelling toward an office on the other side of the street. He was calling someone by name and threatening him. He accused the man of something, Steele didn't understand just what, and he called him a long string of vile epithets. Soon the office door across the street opened, and a tall man in a black suit stepped out onto the board sidewalk. He had shoulder-length hair, a black handlebar moustache and a long, slim cigar between his lips. He was wearing a wide-brimmed, low-crowned hat. His manner was calm. The name caller in the street shouted, "I'm going to kill you, you no good sonofabitch," and he raised his revolver and fired a shot which broke a window behind the cigar smoker's back. A second shot splintered the sidewalk at the tall man's feet. The tall man then, it seemed, very slowly and deliberately withdrew his pistol from its holster, raised it up to shoulder level and fully extended his arm. Another shot from the street went wild. Steele couldn't tell where that one went. Then the man on the sidewalk pulled the trigger—once. The bullet hit the name caller in the street right square in the middle of the forehead. From his vantage point behind the victim, Steele could see the blood and brains squirt out the back of his skull. He saw the head jerk back, the rest of the body go limp. He saw the man fall backward, land in the dirt street with a dull thud, bounce once, then settle down, his head resting in a slowly expanding pool of dark, red ooze. He looked across the street then and saw the man in the black suit calmly holster his gun, turn and walk back into the office. Steele was fascinated.

He wasn't one to enjoy a sight such as he had just seen. He was no sadist. He did not particularly like killing, though, he thought, he had done some of it himself and would readily admit that there were some people in the world who probably needed killing. No, it hadn't been watching a man get killed that had gripped Steele's attention so. It hadn't been watching a man die or seeing the blood. The thing that had so held Steele's attention had been the manner of the victorious gunfighter. The man had played, he thought, a brilliant role. He wondered if it might be a role he could play.

Before the company left St. Joseph, Steele had bought himself a pistol. It was a brand-new model from Colt, an 1873 Peacemaker with a seven-and-a-half-inch barrel. It had smooth handgrips made of dark wood. A beautiful tool, Steele thought. When the company camped on the road between towns, he would wander away from the camp and practice with his pistol. He was fascinated by the character of the gunfighter, and like an actor taking on a new role, he rehearsed it with every opportunity. His walk and his stance, which before had been based on the classical roles he had played on the stage, changed. He imitated the westerners he observed. His speech when not on the stage began to change as well. When the company arrived at a new town, Blue Steele could go out on his own into a saloon, and though he might be noticed as a stranger, he would not be taken for one of the company of actors that was known to have just arrived in town.

It seemed as if the whole town of Riddle, Iowa, turned out to watch the caravan of theater wagons as it drove through on its way to the Missouri River crossing. Ragamuffin kids ran alongside the wagons. Dogs chased the horses and the wagon wheels.

"What kind of players are ye?" shouted an old farmer.

"Shakespearean, sir," answered Seagraves from his seat in the lead wagon.

"What's that?" said the farmer.

A man in a business suit hurried to the edge of the street.

"You going to play Shakespeare here in Riddle?"

"We've been engaged to play West Riddle, Nebraska, sir," said Seagraves. "No one asked us to play Riddle."

"They going to West Riddle?" said the farmer.

"That's what he said," replied the businessman, then he shouted after Seagraves. "Come back across and play for us when you're done with them across the river."

"If ye survive West Riddle," said the farmer.

Seagraves hauled up his team, set the brake and turned in his seat to face the businessman.

"Are you serious, sir?"

"I sure am. We don't get much in the way of entertainment around here. Especially anything of an intellectual nature."

"But, sir, we'll be playing just across the river. You folks can cross right over for the play."

"No," said the businessman. "We don't go over into West

Riddle. You finish up over there and then come and play over here for us."

"It just happens that we have the time on our schedule to allow us to do that, but I'd have to have a commitment on paper, and we need a hall."

"I can arrange all that for you. If you don't have time to get down right now and deal with me, come back across during the day when you're not playing, and I'll have everything all arranged. We can sign the papers then."

"How will I find you, sir?"

"My name is Coleman Miller, sir. You can find me most anytime at Miller's Emporium, right over there. My establishment."

Miller extended his hand, and Seagraves leaned down from his wagon seat to grasp it.

"Pleased to meet you, Mr. Miller," he said. "My name's Seagraves, Brice Seagraves. I'm the owner and manager of this traveling company of thespians, and the senior member of the cast and crew. I'll be back around to see you, sir. Right now my business across the river is pressing. Good day."

"Good day to you, Mr. Seagraves," said Miller.

"And good luck in West Riddle," added the farmer. "You'll be needing it."

Blue Steele overheard the conversation from his spot in the second wagon, and he wondered what the old farmer had meant by his ominous-sounding remarks. It could be nothing. It could be just the manner of the midwestern farmer. Or it could be that the audience in West Riddle would be a hard one to please. That was all right. He had played to tough houses before. But why did Miller want them to drive back across the river to do a show? Why not, as Seagraves had suggested, just drive over to see it in West Riddle? Civic pride perhaps? Or was something wrong over in West Riddle, Nebraska? Well, they would soon find out. The wagon lurched up onto the river bridge, and

Steele listened to the drone of the wagon wheels and the hollow-sounding clops of the horses' hooves as they crossed the wide Missouri River into the suddenly mysterious town of West Riddle, Nebraska.

Soon the wagons had all halted on the main street of the town, and just as on the Iowa side, they had attracted a curious crowd. Seagraves climbed stiffly and painfully down from his wagon-seat perch. He stretched his limbs. A rough-looking man in a dust-covered black suit with two pistols at his hips stepped forward. He spoke to Seagraves with a cigar clenched in his teeth.

"You must be the actors we been looking for," he said.

"Seagraves is the name, sir. I have business with Mr. Overton Avant."

"Yeah, well, Avant sent me. They call me Alfalfa George. You come with me, and I'll show you the the-ayter."

Alfalfa George didn't wait for a response but started walking down the sidewalk without a backward glance. Seagraves called over his shoulder to his actors still in the wagons as he hurried after George.

"Climb down and stretch your legs, folks. Take a rest. I'll be back shortly to get us settled in."

Alfalfa George led Seagraves down the street to a large saloon. Inside Seagraves saw that the saloon looked as he would have expected on one side of a large room. That is, it had a long ornate bar with a large mirror on the wall behind it, and out front, tables for sitting and drinking or for playing cards, and roulette tables. But the other side of the room, equally large, was a theater.

"Over there's the stage," said George. "That's where you'll do your playacting. Follow me."

Blue Steele walked into the saloon just in time to see Seagraves follow George to the bar. He walked on over to join them. The other members of the cast came in behind him. The ladies found a table. The men went straight to the bar and ordered a bottle and some glasses which they then took to the table to enjoy with the ladies. Blue Steele stayed at the bar near Seagraves and ordered a shot of rye whiskey. He thought about ordering a bottle, but he was low on cash. He was looking forward to payday at the end of the West Riddle engagement. He tossed down the drink and listened to Alfalfa George.

"Blanch," said George.

A woman behind the bar turned to face George. She was in her early thirties, Steele guessed. Her blond hair was piled high on top of her head, and her makeup was heavy. Heavy enough for the stage, thought Steele. Even so, she was still a fine-looking woman.

"What is it, George?" she said.

"Them actors is here. This here is, uh . . ."

"Brice Seagraves, ma'am," said the old manager, extending his hand to the lady.

She took his hand in hers and Seagraves bent to kiss it.

"A great pleasure, ma'am," he said.

"Why, thank you," she said. "What a pleasure it is to have a real gentleman around this town for a change."

Blanch shot a meaningful look at Alfalfa George with her last remark. If her meaning soaked in, George gave no indication.

"You take care of him, Blanch," he said. "I got things to do."

"Sure," said Blanch to George's back as he moved toward the door. She turned back to Seagraves. "You want to rest and freshen up a bit before we get down to business? I'll be here all evening."

As Blanch came out from behind the bar, she passed by Steele and gave him a glance. As she did, he tipped his hat. Then he fell in behind Seagraves as the old man followed Blanch up the stairs to the rooms which she had waiting for the actors. Steele hadn't been invited along. The rest of the actors sat and drank while their manager took care of business and made preparations for them. But Steele did

not like the feeling of West Riddle, and though he had
been taken away from it at an early age, his Cherokee
upbringing had instilled in him a respect for his elders. He
felt compelled to look after the older man. Seagraves did
not meet Overton Avant that night. He conducted his
business entirely with Blanch Storey, who, he discovered,
owned the saloon and theater. The following morning, the
company rehearsed *Macbeth* in the theater before the
saloon was open for business. Everything was ready for an
evening performance. They slept the rest of the day away
and came to the theater in the evening ready for a rousing
show. Steele wore a shaggy wig and beard for his part of
Macduff. He made even the tough-looking plainsmen in
the audience weep when he cried, "What, all my pretty
chickens and their dam at one fell swoop?" And in the final
scene when he encountered Macbeth and growled rather
than spoke the line "Turn, Hellhound, turn," they shouted
cheers and encouragement to him until he had finally
defeated the hated tyrant with his broadsword and lifted
high into the air the stage-prop head of Macbeth dripping
blood. For all the shortness of his part, he was the hero to
this crowd. They played to a full house, and Seagraves paid
everybody. The next day, they put the money back into
circulation in West Riddle.

The following night they played *Romeo and Juliet,* again
to a full house. The audience was a bit rowdy, yes, but
generally highly appreciative. Seagraves and Steele both
wondered what the remarks of the Iowa farmer had been
all about. Things were going well in West Riddle. They
could hardly have been any better. The following morning, Seagraves had everyone up early to pack the wagons.
Alfalfa George appeared on the sidewalk. He was wearing
the same dusty black suit he had worn two days before.

"You look like you're fixing to leave town or something,"
he said.

"Yes," said Seagraves. "We contracted to perform two

plays, *Macbeth* and *Romeo and Juliet,* and we've done them both. Now we'll be on our way."

"Not yet you won't," said George.

"I beg your pardon," said Seagraves.

"Avant just come into town this morning. He ain't seen them plays yet, and he's the one ordered them. You're going to do them again."

"Well, I . . ."

Seagraves had started to say that they had other obligations, but he knew that to be a lie. He looked at Alfalfa George whose eyes seemed to have narrowed to slits. George's hands were resting on his pistol butts.

"I, uh, yes," said Seagraves. "We can play it again."

"Both of them," said George. "One tonight and one tomorrer."

"Yes. Of course."

Blue Steele went back into the saloon after he had helped to unpack the wagons which they had just a little earlier packed thinking that they were leaving town. The saloon was opened, but there were no customers. It was still early in the day. The bartender had gone out back to get some fresh bottles for his bar stock, so when Steele leaned on the bar, Blanch moved around behind it.

"Can I get something for you, Mr. Hamlin?" she asked.

"Rye whiskey," said Steele. That was one part of J. B. Temple that Steele hadn't been able to put behind him— the craving for rye whiskey. Blanch put a shot glass on the bar, then slid a bottle up beside it.

"So you're staying a couple of more days?" she said.

"It looks that way," said Steele, tossing down the drink and pouring himself another from the bottle. "Who is this Avant anyway?"

Blanch laughed.

"Overton Avant just about owns West Riddle, Mr. Hamlin. I own this place and Charlie Lewis down the road owns the stable, but Overton owns just about everything else. He runs things here his own way."

"We just found that out."

"Oh, don't worry about it. You'll have the whole town out to see the plays again, even if they have seen them before. We don't get things like this around here very often. They'll come back. You'll make plenty of money on it."

"I suppose you're right," said Steele. "We've done all right so far."

He poured one more drink and swallowed it, then paid Blanch.

"Well," he said, "we got up too early this morning anyway. I think I'll go back to bed."

"Mr. Hamlin," said Blanch, "I've got some girls here. Nice young ones. You want me to send one up to you? They usually don't work this time of day, but I could get ahold of one of them if you like."

Steele stopped. He was suddenly filled with revulsion at Blanch, her hotel and saloon and the whole town of West Riddle.

"I don't buy women," he said, and he went on upstairs, took off his coat, shirt and boots and lay across the bed.

Well, he thought, *two days more or less shouldn't make a difference. Where am I going anyway?*

CHAPTER FOUR

While Steele napped, Seagraves rented a saddle horse and took a ride across the Missouri River bridge into Riddle, Iowa, where he looked up Coleman Miller. Miller invited Seagraves for a drink in a local saloon. They got a bottle and sat at a table by the window.

"Mr. Miller," Seagraves began, "I've been engaged for two more nights across the river at the insistence of Mr. Avant. I can bring my company into your town immediately after that. Have you located a suitable hall?"

"Yes, I have, Mr. Seagraves," said Miller. "We're looking forward to your stint here in our town. I hope the hall will be satisfactory. I'll show it to you in a few minutes. We've never had Shakespeare here in Riddle."

Seagraves took a long drink.

"There's something strange about that town across the river, Mr. Miller," he said. "I wondered when we came through here why your people couldn't just trot across the bridge to see the plays. I wondered why you were so insistent about having us come back over here. I still don't know—exactly—but it's a strange town."

"Mr. Seagraves," said Miller, "we've got a decent town here with a good town marshal and a county sheriff. We've got honest, hard-working folks here. But that river's the dividing line. It's the boundary between Iowa and Nebraska. Our jurisdiction ends right smack in the middle of that bridge. And West Riddle is a wide-open town run by Overton Avant, as crooked a hound as you'll ever run across. He's a thorn in our side. He's an embarrassment to our community, and there's nothing we'd rather do than ride over there and clean that place up once and for all. But there's nothing we can do."

"Is everything over there crooked?"

"I think that most of the citizens are decent enough folks," said Miller, "but Avant and his thugs keep everything under their control. The others are afraid to make a move."

"Well," sighed Seagraves, scratching his head in disbelief at the situation he found himself in, "I'll be just as glad to get my whole company over here on your side of the river and leave Mr. Overton Avant and his town far behind me."

Seagraves emptied his glass as a third man walked over to the table where he and Miller sat. The man wore a badge on his vest and a six-gun on his hip. He was a big, rugged-looking man with a heavy red moustache. He gave Miller a friendly slap on the back.

"Oh," said Miller, looking over his shoulder, "hello, Bluff."

"Howdy, Coleman," said the newcomer.

"Mr. Seagraves," said Miller, "I'd like you to meet Bluff Luton, our town marshal. Bluff, this is Brice Seagraves. He's in charge of that bunch of actors that came through here the other day."

"How do you do, sir?" said Seagraves offering his hand.

"Howdy, Seagraves," said Luton, shaking his hand. "You over in West Riddle still?"

"For two more nights unfortunately," said Seagraves, "then, happily, we'll be coming here to your town, and I don't mind telling you that it will be a great relief to be in a town with reliable law enforcement."

"We do our best."

The bartender yelled from across the room.

"Hey, Sarge, you want a drink?"

Luton called back over his shoulder.

"No, thanks, Gabe," he said. "Too early in the day for me."

"Sergeant?" said Seagraves, a puzzled look on his face.

"Oh," said Luton, smiling, "I was in the army. Some folks just can't seem to stop calling me Sergeant even though I been town marshal here for eight years now."

"Bluff," said Miller, "I was just about to show Mr. Seagraves the hall I've arranged for his performances. Care to join us?"

"Sure, I'll walk along with you."

Miller turned to Seagraves.

"You want to take a look at that hall now?"

"Let's do that," said Seagraves, "and I can tell you that I'm already looking forward to moving my productions into it."

The three men left the saloon together.

That night in West Riddle Blue Steele played a fiery Mercutio. When he challenged Tybalt and fought with him, the crowd roared, and when he died, cursing both the houses of Montague and Capulet, there were not many dry eyes in the crowd. He was removing his makeup backstage when Blanch walked in. He was not pleased at the intrusion. He remembered the last time a lady had come into his dressing room.

"You did a fine job as usual," she said.

"Thank you," said Steele. "Who was that portly gentleman I saw you sitting with?"

"Oh," said Blanch, "that was Overton Avant."

"I thought perhaps that was he," replied Steele. "So the king has finally made his appearance."

He recalled the paunchy man he had seen sitting beside Blanch in the front row of theater seats, slightly gray at the temples, bald on top, a thin moustache, wearing a very expensive suit. He had smoked a slim cigar throughout the performance and had kept a waiter busy bringing him drinks. Steele didn't like the man. He didn't like his looks. He didn't like his arrogance.

"He liked the play," said Blanch.

"And he sent you with the message? How very kind of him."

Steele finished washing his face and changing his clothes. Then he went out to the bar and ordered a shot of rye whiskey. Blanch was milling around with customers. Steele looked the room over, but Avant was nowhere to be seen. He casually wondered where the man might have gone. Alfalfa George with Benjamin Goree, another of Avant's hired guns, was lounging against the far wall, his coat pushed back to reveal the two pistols hanging at his sides. Steele finished a third shot of rye whiskey and went to the roulette table. He put five dollars on the black and watched the wheel spin. He lost. He put down another five and this time watched the wheel more closely. Again he lost, but, he thought, the wheel had a peculiar way of coming to a stop. He put down a third bet and this time watched the wheel's operator. Steele could perceive a slight movement as if the operator had nudged a lever under the table with his leg.

"That's enough for me," he said. "This wheel's a bit eccentric."

Alfalfa George stepped forward menacingly, his hands on his pistol butts.

"What do you mean by that, Actor?" he said.

"Excuse me? By what?" said Steele.

"That there word you said—what's it mean?"

"Oh, that," said Steele. "Nothing. This game is strange to me. I've never played it before. I don't understand it."

Alfalfa George, a suspicious look on his face, nodded and grunted in a futile attempt to show that he had understood Steele. Steele thought that he would like to draw on this man. He would like to kill him. He found the thought amusing. He had not intended to kill Chester back in New

York, and he hadn't enjoyed killing Chester. He did not pride himself on the killing of Chester. It was just something that had happened, and it was unfortunate. And even when he had been filled with righteous indignation, rage and bitter hatred for Gill and Dillon, when he, personally, had been brutally beaten and humiliated, he had not wanted to kill. But this man, this Alfalfa George, he would like to kill. He knew that he was fast and accurate with a six-gun, but he had never faced a gunfighter before. He didn't really know what it would be like. He didn't know how fast he would be in comparison to others—to real gunfighters.

He went back to the bar for one more shot. Looking around the room, he noticed that Blanch was no longer in sight. He polished off the drink and went up to his room. He shut the door behind him, took the key from his pocket, locked the door and tossed the key on the table. He undressed and went to bed, but he didn't sleep right away. He kept thinking about Avant and Alfalfa George and the general tension of West Riddle. Eventually he dropped off to sleep.

The next day Steele spent mostly in his room with a bottle of rye whiskey. That night he played the most furious Macduff of his career. Poor Guymon Adams, as Macbeth, was actually frightened at the power and rage in Steele's blows with the broadsword. Avant and Blanch sat again in the front row. After the final curtain, the actors had barely had time to get out of makeup and costumes when Seagraves had them packing to leave West Riddle. Makeup, costumes, props and set pieces were packed up and loaded into the wagons. Actors packed their personal belongings and loaded them. The horses were hitched to the wagons. Seagraves, with the profits from the four nights in West Riddle in a box under his arm, was about to climb onto the bench of the lead wagon when he felt a hand on his shoulder.

"Not so fast, Mr. Actor-man," said Alfalfa George. "We've got a little business to conduct."

"Our business is concluded, sir. We've performed not only the two shows we contracted for but two additional ones as well. Our bills are paid, and we have our share of the receipts."

"There's more to it than that," said George.

"More?"

"That's right. Let's go back inside. And bring that there cash box with you."

Seagraves hesitated. Alfalfa George flipped back his coattails and gripped his pistols. Goree and another thug stepped up beside him. Seagraves sighed, hugged his cashbox and followed George inside. Steele started to climb down from the second wagon, but George turned and pointed a finger at him as if it were a pistol.

"Ain't no need for you to come along, Macduffy," he said.

Steele settled back into the wagon, anger boiling up inside him. He wondered what Alfalfa George was up to. Was he going to make them stay longer and perform again? Had he let them pack up again only to make them unpack as before? What kind of game was Alfalfa George playing with them? Or rather, what kind of game was Overton Avant playing? Steele was convinced that Alfalfa George was no more than Avant's yes-man, his lackey, a hired thug. He thought again about strapping on his own six-gun and facing George, but Goree and the other man were standing just outside the front entrance to Blanch's saloon facing the wagons. Steele clenched his teeth and waited, but as it turned out, the wait wasn't really very long.

Seagraves came rushing out the front door, his face red with anger and frustration, with Alfalfa George hard on his heels. Seagraves hurried to the lead wagon and quickly climbed aboard. George let out a raucous laugh.

"Let's go," shouted Seagraves, lashing at his horses. "Let's get out of here. Away, away, away."

And he raced his lead wagon toward the Missouri River bridge, the other wagons following as fast as they could with Alfalfa George and his two sidekicks firing shots over their heads and laughing uproariously. Seagraves didn't slow down until he was safely on the Iowa side of the river. The wagons all stopped along the main street of Riddle. Seagraves set his brake and then dropped his head in his hands. He made no move to climb down. The rest of the company piled out of the wagons and gathered around the old man.

"What was that all about?" asked Eva Knowles, who played both Juliet and Lady Macbeth.

"What happened back there?" said Adams.

Seagraves raised his hands to silence them.

"I'll explain everything in the hotel," he said. "Mr. Miller has got us all rooms here. Right now we've got to get these horses and wagons taken care of."

Soon the company was gathered in the hotel lobby. Seagraves produced a bottle and handed it around.

"We're almost broke again," he said.

"How could that be?" said Adams.

"Keep quiet," said Steele, "and give the man a chance to tell us."

Seagraves turned his pockets inside out and let a few bills and coins fall out onto a table.

"This is all that's left," he said. "At gunpoint, the man demanded that I pay a tax on money earned. He said he was West Riddle's tax collector. I paid him. Then he said that we had played without a license, and that West Riddle has an ordinance which requires traveling players to obtain a license before putting on shows. I paid him for the license. Then the filthy knave said that we owed a fine for having played without the license. I protested that I had just paid the license fee, but he said that I had paid for it after the fact, so we still owed the fine. I paid him again. He's the court clerk, so he said. Finally, he collected rent on the hall as agent for Miss Storey. I told him that Mr. Avant by mail had assured me that everything would be arranged satisfactorily, but that bloody, bawdy villain said that if I were not satisfied I could complain in court on next Wednesday. I decided to count it a lesson well learned and get us all safely out of that den of thieves."

Seagraves paused. He looked old and very tired. He opened his hands and gestured pitifully towards the cash on the table.

"That's all he left us," he said. "I owe all of you money, and I can't pay it, but I promise you that you shall get all you've got coming to you. We'll make up for it here in Riddle. Mr. Miller assures me of good crowds, and though I don't put a penny in my own pocket, I'll see to it that each of you gets your pay not only from Riddle but also for what you did in that rat's nest across the river as well."

Steele stood and put a hand on his old friend's shoulder. He felt the old man's pain as if it were his own. It enraged him to think that anyone could deal with an old man so despicably. *Someone else will get what's coming to him as well,* he thought. Then he turned and left the room without saying a word. Soon he was walking back toward the bridge. He was wearing his pistol belt. His black cloak which he had not worn since leaving New York was thrown over his shoulders, and he was carrying Chester's knurly walking stick. It was a dark night, but still Steele was careful to avoid being seen. He wasn't at all sure what he would do, but he was determined that something would be done. Something had to be done. He walked deliberately, carrying the stick in his right hand. As he reached the center of the bridge, the dividing line, he paused. There was chaos before him. Behind him was order. He could see no one across the river, but the lights were still burning in the saloons along the main street of West Riddle. He continued on his walk. Stepping off the bridge in West Riddle, Steele headed for the darkest shadows and made his way to a black, narrow passage between two buildings directly opposite Blanch's saloon. He waited.

Hiram Washburn had worked a small farm a few miles outside of West Riddle for a number of years. He had paid off his mortgage and had been doing fairly well. He was not rich, but he was making a living. Then Overton Avant had moved to West Riddle and had begun taking it over with the help of Alfalfa George and his thugs. Washburn didn't like what he saw happening in West Riddle, but he didn't spend that much time in town, so he tried to put it out of his mind. He tried to ignore it until the time came when Avant began to covet Washburn's property. Avant had made Washburn an offer on the farm. It wasn't nearly what the farm was worth, Washburn thought, and even if it had been, Washburn wasn't planning to move. Avant had later raised the offer slightly, and Washburn had turned him down again. Then Alfalfa George took over. He began harassing Washburn at every opportunity. He led his hired guns riding horseback across Washburn's fields, trampling his crops. He bullied him when Washburn, on rare occasions, had to go into town for supplies. He cut fences. Finally, when George had Washburn's entire crop destroyed and his pigs killed, Washburn realized that he could no longer hold out. He knew that he was licked, but he couldn't relish the thought of allowing Overton Avant to have his way. He had packed up in the middle of the night and headed for Kansas City.

In Kansas City, Washburn had met a man named Hudson. Hudson had only recently arrived from Virginia with his wife and two small children. His Virginia farm was past producing, and he was looking for more fertile land out west. He was in the market for a farm. Washburn failed to inform Hudson about conditions in West Riddle. He did not tell the man about the interest of Overton Avant in his property. He simply described the farm to the unsuspecting Hudson, showed him the deed and made him what sounded to Hudson like a very good offer. The price was still less than what Washburn thought his farm was worth, but he needed to get rid of it quickly, and it was more than Avant's highest offer. Hudson paid for the farm, pocketed the deed, loaded his family into his wagon and headed for his newly acquired property just outside of West Riddle, Nebraska. He had high hopes. He had visions of a new beginning in the west. And when he arrived at the farm, he was not disappointed. It seemed to be in good shape. There were repairs needed, of course, but he had expected that. The whole family set to work immediately getting the house in shape, mending fence and putting in a new crop. It was a month before Hudson found the time or the need to make the trip into West Riddle. He went in alone in his wagon. He first went to the general store for some supplies he needed. Once his business was taken care of, he decided to pamper himself a bit. He stopped in at Blanch's saloon and had a few drinks. Then he sat in on a poker game. A few drinks, he told himself, could do no harm, and he might accidentally win some money. He would keep his bets small, though, in case he should lose. After all, he had his family's welfare to keep in mind.

Hudson won the first few small pots and was feeling good. Then he began to lose, but by then he had forgotten his resolve to play only a few hands. The few pots he had won had drawn him into the game so that all other thoughts left his mind. Soon he had lost all of his earlier winnings and began to lose the money he had started with. Then he began watching the dealer more closely. He thought that he saw a card dealt from the bottom of the deck. It had been a fast and tricky move, and he wasn't sure. But he thought that the card had come from the bottom. Hudson was no fool. He kept quiet. He waited until the hand was played out and he had lost again. He discovered that he was broke. He wanted to accuse the dealer, but he wasn't positive. He thought that he should probably simply leave—take it as a lesson learned the hard way, go home and confess his foolishness to his wife. He slowly pushed his chair back from the table and stood up.

"Well," he said, "that cleans me out. I guess I'm through."

But he didn't leave. He was thinking that if he just walked out of this place, he would be known as a fool. He had been cheated, and he wanted to call the dealer on it. So he just stepped back a little from the table and continued watching the game. He would catch that crooked dealer in the act. He was standing with his back to the big window which looked out onto the street. At a table against the wall to Hudson's right but some distance across the room sat Overton Avant. He was watching Hudson. Avant raised a fat, pink finger and crooked it toward Alfalfa George who stood in his usual position lounging against the wall. George sauntered over to Avant.

"You see that fella over there by the window, George?" said Avant, nodding his head toward Hudson.

"Yeah."

"He looks like a troublemaker. He just lost all his money in that poker game. He looks to me like a bad loser."

"Yeah," said George. "What's he hanging around like that for if he's broke?"

"He's trying to catch Silky at something," said Avant. "He's going to try to make some trouble. Blanch don't need no trouble in here, George."

"Yeah, that's right."

George started to walk away from the table and toward the window, but Avant caught him by the coat sleeve.

"By the way, George," he said, "that's the fella that bought the old Washburn place. Did you know that?"

Bluford Steele stood in the shadows across the street from Blanch's saloon waiting. He was still not certain what he intended to do. He had decided that he was waiting for someone—Alfalfa George or Overton Avant—someone to leave the saloon. Something had to be done, but he would have to be careful. He was no gunfighter—at least not yet. And even if he were, there were too many of them in West Riddle for one man to take them on alone. He didn't even know how many thugs worked under Alfalfa George for Overton Avant. He would have to be careful—and patient. He waited.

Steele was suddenly startled by the loud blast of a gunshot. He flinched at the sound and looked up just in time to see the body of Hudson flying backward through the big window in front of Blanch's saloon. Hudson landed half in the street and half on the sidewalk with a sickening thud and in the midst of the sound of shattering glass. The broken window was immediately filled with curious faces.

"God damn," said one of the curious. "Blowed his face out."

Alfalfa George stepped out onto the sidewalk, his sixgun still in his hand. He looked casually down at what had been Hudson as he loaded a bullet back into the empty chamber. Two or three other onlookers stepped out, followed by Overton Avant who brushed them out of his way as he walked up beside Alfalfa George and put an arm around his shoulder.

"Too bad you had to do that, George," he said, "but that fellow there was just looking for trouble. You got all the witnesses you need to attest to that."

George holstered the pistol.

"You've put in a long day," Avant continued. "Why

don't you go on home and get some sleep? We'll take care of everything here. Go on."

George started walking diagonally across the street. His path would lead him to the corner at the far end of the block on the same side of the street as was Steele. Steele turned and made his way through the dark passage to behind the buildings, then headed for the end of the block by way of the alley in order to intercept Alfalfa George. He couldn't have planned it better. George was alone. It was dark. George was walking right into an ambush that Steele had only in a very general sense planned. Steele moved as fast as he could while trying to keep quiet and out of sight. He reached the end of the block, and pressing his back against the back wall of the corner building, slowly and carefully eased toward the edge to peer around the corner. He saw Alfalfa George coming. He hefted the knurly walking stick in his right hand with a grip about two thirds of the way down. The top of the stick formed a solid knob. Steele's heart began to pound in anticipation of the act which he contemplated. He thought for an instant that Alfalfa George would hear the pounding. Then George was right beside him, totally unaware of his presence. Steele let George take two more long strides before he stepped out of the shadow of the alley right behind him, the stick raised high in the air. His first impulse was to bring the stick crashing down onto the back of George's head, but the arrogance of John B. Temple overcame him. He wanted George to know. Maintaining his poised position, he spoke softly into the night.

"Turn, hellhound, turn," he said.

Alfalfa George started to spin quickly around as his right hand almost automatically reached for the six-gun at his right side.

"Macduffy," he said.

He had recognized his assailant, turned about halfway around and thumbed back the hammer of the pistol, which was still only halfway out of the holster, when the knob of the knurly stick caught him between the eyes, crushing the bones of the nose, the lower forehead and the eye sockets. George fell back heavily, his head slamming against the hard ground last and bouncing once causing the blood to splash through the splintered bones. Steele had raised the stick again in anticipation of a second blow, but even in the darkness he could see that there was no need for another. He looked around himself quickly. Then he knelt over the body and went quickly through the pockets. Of course, George didn't have Seagraves' money on him. It had been a foolish hope. He would have turned that over to Avant right away after having deprived Seagraves of it. He did have some cash on him, though, and Steele took it. It would help Seagraves out some until Steele could find a way to recover the money from the cash box. He tossed the empty wallet back down. That would be just fine. It would look like a common robbery. It was a robbery, of course, but it was anything but a common one. It was justice for Seagraves and his entire company. It was also personal. Steele had wanted to kill Alfalfa George. He felt differently standing over the body of Alfalfa George from what he had felt in New York standing over that of Chester. This felt good. It was just and right and proper. He stuffed the cash into his pocket, knelt once more over the body and carefully cleaned the knob of the knurly stick on George's coattails. He stood up, looked around once more, and started walking back down the alley, back toward the river bridge and the dividing line.

Across the street in dark shadows, a young cowboy stood with a freshly rolled cigarette between his lips and a match in his hand, poised to strike. He had stopped himself from striking the match when he saw Steele step out of the alley and raise his stick behind George. He had stood there in the dark, silent, a witness to the entire scene.

CHAPTER FIVE

When Steele returned to Riddle, he found the town quiet. It was late, and the saloon was just about to close. There were only a couple of customers left in the place. He went to the bar and paid for a bottle of rye whiskey, then went to the hotel and up to his room. After a few drinks, he fell into a deep but fitful sleep. Images of violence filled his head. He saw once again the fateful shooting of Chickenhawk, and once again he was the half-breed child, Blue Steele. He was Blue Steele still, frustrated in love and stomped by the ruffians of New Hampshire. And he was Blue Steele choking those same ruffians on their own rope and leaving New Hampshire behind him in flames. He was King Richard being hacked to pieces on Bosworth Field, and then, suddenly, he was John Berringer Temple fighting desperately to ward off the vicious strokes of Chester's knurly stick. He plunged the dagger once again into Chester's soft belly flesh and watched again the blood flow out onto the dressing room floor. He saw again the gunfight in St. Joseph, watched the loser fly backward and fall to the ground, saw the victor casually turn and go back into the office. Then he was the victorious gunfighter, a pistol on each hip, notches on the handles. Alfalfa George reappeared and once again blasted the farmer through the front window of Blanch's saloon, and Steele smashed his face in—again and again.

It was late the next morning when Steele woke up. Wet from sweat, he sat on the edge of the bed. *Who am I?* he

asked himself. *Just who the hell am I? Blue Steele? John B.
Temple? Tyrone Hamlin? Or somebody else altogether?
Indian or white? Does it really even matter?* He stood up
and walked to the basin of water on the table below a
mirror. He splashed his face with lukewarm, stale water,
then dried it on a towel and looked up into the mirror.

"I can be anything I want to be," he said. "I can be
anybody. I am an actor."

He stood up straight and postured for himself, then began to recite.

> "Why, I can smile, and murder whiles I
>   smile,
> And cry 'content' to that which grieves my
>   heart,
> And wet my cheeks with artificial tears,
> And frame my face to all occasions.
>
> ———
>
> I can add colors to the chameleon,
> Change shapes with Proteus for advantages,
> And set the murderous Machiavel to
>   school."

Feeling better, he dressed and went downstairs to find
something to eat. In the hotel's dining room, he found
Brice Seagraves sitting alone over a cup of coffee. Steele
joined him and ordered a breakfast of ham and eggs. Sipping his coffee with Seagraves, Steele felt the bulge in his
vest pocket. He was all of a sudden in a jovial mood.

"I read somewhere," he said, "that on the morning he
inherited his title and estates, Lord Byron had a breakfast
of ham and eggs and beer. All I'm missing is the beer. I
think I'll order one."

Seagraves raised his heavy eyebrows to look at Steele.
"What's your occasion?" he asked.

Steele reached inside his vest pocket and produced the

cash he had taken off the body of Alfalfa George the night before and with a small flourish, he tossed it on the table.

"It isn't all you lost, Brice," he said, "but it should help."

"I won't take your money, Johnny," said Seagraves. "I owe you already."

"This isn't my money," said Steele, a wry smile on his lips. "And I don't know what else to do with it, so it's yours."

"Where did you get this?"

Steele looked around the room. There was no one to overhear. If there had been, Seagraves would never have called him by his other name. The old man had been very careful about that. Steele sipped his coffee.

"Brice," he said, his voice low, "I murdered Alfalfa George last night. I walked back across the bridge, I hid outside the saloon and I ambushed him when he came out. I bashed his face in with the stick of that blasted Chester I killed in New York. Then I took this money off his body. So it's all right. He took your money, and I took his, and now I'm giving you his money to partially make up for what he stole from you. He wasn't carrying your cash on him. I expect that he had already given that up to his employer, that weaselly Avant. Anyway, this should help you with the expenses, pay for the others to keep them happy, whatever, until you can make some profits from the next performance."

"But what about you?"

"I still have a bit of my own money. I'm doing all right."

"But you've killed a man."

"I've done that before. Remember?"

"J. B. Temple killed a man in New York," said Seagraves, "and he's a fugitive from justice. You had to take on a new identity. Now Tyrone Hamlin has killed a man in Nebraska."

"I was careful not to be seen, Brice. Stop worrying."

"But suppose they find out somehow. Suppose you were seen."

"Tyrone Hamlin came about rather easily," said Steele. "I'm an actor. I can change roles as easily as most men change clothes. I think perhaps I've hung onto you for too long anyway, Brice. It's about time for me to move on."

"Will you play the shows in Riddle?"

"I'll play Mercutio for you tonight and Macduff tomorrow. It would look bad for me to disappear before the shows anyway. In the meantime, old boy, work something out to get along without me. I may be moving along rather unexpectedly."

A cowboy came into the room and sat at a table across from Steele. While he waited for the waiter to come around to take his order, he rolled a cigarette and lit it. He was watching Steele. Steele and Seagraves both saw the cowboy come in and decided without mentioning it to each other to change the subject. About that same time, Steele's breakfast arrived. Seagraves ordered himself a refill of coffee and Steele ordered his beer. The waiter stopped by the cowboy's table on his way back to the bar, and the cowboy ordered coffee. Steele glanced toward the cowboy occasionally, and each time he did so, he had the feeling that the cowboy had been staring at him but had just glanced away to avoid his look. Steele began to feel a bit uneasy. Then the cowboy stood up and walked over toward Steele and Seagraves.

"Howdy," he said.

"How do you do, sir," said Seagraves.

Steele looked at the cowboy for a moment.

"Howdy," he said.

"You fellers actors?" said the cowboy.

"We are indeed," said Seagraves.

"I kinda thought so. I seen the signs up around town. What you doing tonight?"

"*Romeo and Juliet* tonight. Curtain at eight."

"Where can I get a ticket?"

"Tickets will be available at the door," said Seagraves. "But come a little early if you want a good seat. We expect a crowd."

The cowboy shuffled his feet and scratched his head. He was looking down at the table, not at Seagraves or Steele.

"I'll do that," he said. "Uh, they call me Neosho."

He thrust his hand out between the other two men, and Seagraves stood up. He took Neosho's hand and pumped it vigorously.

"Brice Seagraves, sir," he said. "Manager of this troupe of traveling players. Pleased to make your acquaintance, Mr. Neosho."

"Oh, it don't take mister in front of it," said Neosho. He looked toward Steele.

Steele daubed at his mouth with his napkin, pushed his chair back from the table and stood up slowly, looking hard into Neosho's face the whole time. Then he extended his hand.

"Tyrone Hamlin," he said.

Neosho shook the hand.

"Well," he said, "I'll be seeing you tonight."

"I'm sure," said Steele.

Neosho tipped his hat and ambled out of the room. Steele and Seagraves exchanged questioning looks. Neither one, however, had anything appropriate to say. Steele sat back down and dug into his breakfast, but although he did not mention anything more about Neosho to Seagraves, or to anyone else, he was bothered by the man. He believed that Neosho had been staring at him for some minutes before he came over to introduce himself. Why had the cowboy been staring at him? What interest had he in Steele? What interest had he in theater, for that matter, especially in Shakespearean theater? And who was this Neosho? What the hell kind of a name was that? A cowboy. A cowboy with a funny name and an interest in actors or in

theater or in Shakespeare? No, thought Steele. Neosho was
a cowboy with an interest in Steele, for some reason. But
what was the reason? What was the source of his interest?
Steele felt that he had not seen the last of this Neosho, and
that thought irritated him.

Just as Steele was finishing his breakfast of ham and eggs
and beer, there was a great commotion in the street. Seagraves jumped from his seat and ran to the window. Steele
glanced toward the window with mild curiosity but made
no move. *The old man can be pretty lively when he wants
to be,* he thought. He gulped the last of his beer.

"What is it?" he asked.

"Oh, I see," said Seagraves. "It's the stagecoach coming
in. Let's go out and watch."

"I'm not sure what there is to watch, Brice," said Steele,
"but I'll join you."

The stagecoach pulling into Riddle was obviously a major event in the life of the town. It seemed to Steele as if
everyone in town must have been out in the street. There
were people looking for mail, people looking for passen-
gers and people just looking at the arrival of the stage
because it was something different for them to do with
themselves. Sergeant Bluff Luton was questioning the
driver about the trip, which apparently had been totally
uneventful.

"That's good," said Luton. "That's the best kind of trip."

As the driver carried the mail bags into the post office, a
group of the curious and of the anxious followed him.
Steele thought to himself that if the arrival of the coach
was such an event, the play coming up that night should
really create a stir. That was good for Seagraves. He was
startled out of his thoughts by the touch of a hand on his
shoulder. It was not Seagraves' hand, for the old man was
beside him within the range of his peripheral vision. Steele
looked around and saw Neosho smiling into his face.

"Howdy, Mr. Hamlin,". said the cowboy. "Wonder if I could buy you a drink?"

"I'm in the company of Mr. Seagraves here, sir," said Steele, wondering again what this strange cowboy's interest in him might be.

Seagraves said, "It's all right, Tyrone. Go along and have a drink. I'm just about to go upstairs and get some rest before I have to begin preparations for tonight. Don't mind me."

Steele was irritated. He didn't like the way this fellow was insinuating himself into his life. He was too pushy. What did he want anyway? Steele didn't think that he liked this Neosho, but he was curious, and he figured the only way to satisfy his curiosity would be to accept the offer of a drink.

"Very well," he said. "Where do you like?"

Neosho led Steele to a small saloon on a back street, away from the main part of Riddle. There were only a couple of other customers in the place. Steele wondered if Neosho might have had an interest in this bar and was trying to boost its business. He couldn't think of any other reason to have come there when there were much nicer places on the main street.

"What do you drink?" asked Neosho.

"Rye whiskey," said Steele.

Neosho bought a bottle of rye, got two glasses and led the way to a table in a far corner. It was dark and dingy. The floor was sticky. Steele checked the tabletop. At least it seemed to have been wiped clean lately. They sat down and Neosho poured two drinks from the bottle. He shoved one across the table to Steele.

"Cheers," he said, lifting his glass and smiling.

Steele lifted his glass in response but said nothing. Neosho's smile aggravated him. *What in blazes is this smiling little bastard up to?* he asked himself.

"Mr. Hamlin," said Neosho, "I want to talk to you."

"Well?"

"It ain't easy—what I want to talk about."

"I'm afraid," said Steele, "that I can't make it any easier for you. I haven't the foggiest notion what it is you want to talk about, although I had an idea that you had something in mind concerning me the way you were watching me over my breakfast."

"Oh, yeah. I'm sorry about that," said Neosho. "I wasn't intending to make you uneasy or nothing like that. I, uh, was just trying to figure out how to approach you, you know? Listen. Let me tell you a little something about myself, if you don't mind."

Steele sighed as if he had much better things to do with his time.

"Please do," he said.

Neosho poured two more drinks. If he could read Steele's manner, he chose to ignore it. He leaned forward in his chair, putting both elbows on the table. His eyes looked into his drink, not at Steele. He took a sip of the rye whiskey, and finally he started talking again.

"I'm a cowhand," he said.

"I guessed as much," said Steele.

"Yeah, I reckon it is kind of obvious. Well, I worked for a lot of cow outfits in my time, and you don't make much money punching someone else's cows. But I saved up. I worked hard and I worked long and I saved up. I bought myself a little spread over across the river, and I put a few cows on it, and I figured, give myself a few years and I'd do all right. I didn't ever figure on getting rich, but I'd do all right. Maybe make enough one of these days to find myself a nice little woman and maybe even raise a family, you know? Things looked kind of promising. I wasn't setting the world on fire, but, well, things looked pretty good to me. It don't take a hell of a lot to make a man like me happy. I don't want too much. Just my little share. And I had it."

Neosho paused. He finished his drink, noticed that Steele had done likewise, and refilled the glasses. He was no longer smiling. Steele, by this time, had become very curious. Neosho's attitude seemed to have changed. Steele almost thought that he liked the man, or could like him if he knew more about him. He thought it best to keep quiet and let Neosho get around to telling his story in his own way and at his own pace. Steele tossed down his third drink, and this time he refilled the glasses. Neosho rolled a cigarette and lit it. He took a long drag and exhaled the smoke, leaning back in his chair.

"All I wanted," he continued, "was just my little share. But not everyone's like that. There's a feller over yonder in West Riddle that wants to own everything and everybody. He wants it all. Don't want nobody else to have nothing."

He paused to drain his glass again. He was becoming visibly angry.

"I think I may know to whom you are referring," said Steele.

"Sonofabitch is named Overton Avant," continued Neosho. "Avant has got a bunch of hired guns. Number-one gun is—was—a man called Alfalfa George. A couple of years ago, Avant asked me to go to work for him. I told him I wasn't interested. Then they made me an offer on my place. I guess if I didn't want to work for him, he didn't want me around. He didn't offer me half what the place was worth. But even if they had offered what it was worth, it would a been worth more than that to me. That place was what I wanted out of life. I told them I wouldn't sell for no amount of money.

"Well, they rode off, and I thought that was the end of it. Then somebody run off some of my cows. Hell, I didn't have that many cows to begin with, so when they run some off, it really hurt. I had a mortgage to pay on, too. I'd a had to work punching cows my whole life to save enough

money to have bought that little place outright. I owed on
it, and I needed them cows to make my payments. After
that I set up nights watching what cows I had left. I didn't
want them running off the rest of the bunch. I worked
days and set up nights. This went on for several nights, and
I was beginning to get bleary-eyed and a bit rumpled. I
guess I must of smelled like a polecat and looked like cow
shit.

"Sure enough, one night they come back. I seen them,
and I commenced to blazing away at them with my Win-
chester. I winged one of them. He was reeling in the
saddle. I was drawing a good bead on another one—and by
God, I coulda swore it was Alfalfa George, even though it
was dark and he was some distance away from me—but
anyhow, I was drawing a good bead on him when someone
slipped up behind me and whaled me a good one over the
head. I don't know what happened after that, but when I
come to, and I don't know how long I was out, when I
come to, I was beat all to hell. They must have kicked me
and stomped me all over. I had a couple of busted ribs, and
my head was cut up. My gun hand had been stomped.

"Hell, my cows were all gone. I limped back to my little
shanty and found it burned to the ground. The only thing
they had left me was my horse and saddle. I climbed on
and rode into town to the bank. I told that banker that I
was all washed up, that there wasn't no way I would be
able to pay what I owed, and he might just as well go on
ahead and foreclose right then even though the time
wasn't quite up yet. Then I rode on out of that damn town.
I went back down south where my folks come from. I still
got some folks down there, and I laid up down there while
my bones healed up, and all the time I thought about what
I would do when I come back. I knew I was coming back."

Having told the story, Neosho seemed to relax again.
The anger left his face, and his smile even returned. He
looked up at Steele. Steele poured two more drinks.

"There was a little gal back home," said Neosho. "Whenever I left the first time, she was just a kid. But when I went crawling back, well, she had growed up some. You know? Well, I thought, if I still had my little dream place, this here just might be the gal to take home to it, and then we begun to get a little cozy, and finally she ups and tells me that I don't have to have no nest egg. She said that she'd go anyplace with me. I told her that I'd get another start and then I'd come back for her. I told her that I had something I had to do first. But whenever I finally got ready to leave, she ups and comes along with me, by God. Humph. Hell of a gal. We moved into an old line shack back up in the hills. It's on what used to be my property. Avant's bunch don't even know it's up there. And I just been waiting around and trying to figure my move."

"Why haven't you gone to the authorities?" said Steele.

"Hell, Avant owns all the authorities in West Riddle. Circuit judge comes around now and then, but if there's any cases to be heard, Avant's got all his witnesses bought and paid for by the time the judge comes around. If there was any opposition to him, they've been planted six feet under. All the local authority belongs to Avant. They're either bought or they're scared. There ain't nowhere to turn to."

"Why are you telling me this?" said Steele. "What's your interest in me? I'm just a traveling player."

Neosho tossed down another glass of rye. He looked straight into Steele's eyes for the first time.

"I seen you kill Alfalfa George," he said.

Steele went early to the makeshift dressing room provided at the town hall. He had liked the star's dressing room in New York at Booth's. He hadn't really made use of it long enough to be able to say that he had gotten used to it, but he had liked it. He had felt like he deserved it, too. And he didn't like being crowded into a small room with all the other actors, everyone trying to get on makeup at the same time, others wanting to borrow things out of his personal makeup kit, breathing in the powder from others' face dustings. He went early to get on his makeup, get into costume and tuck his makeup kit safely out of the way. So he was alone. His makeup for Mercutio didn't take much concentration. It was straight makeup—no special effects, no wig, no whiskers—just straight makeup. And it was a good thing, too, because Steele's mind was not on the performance ahead of him. His mind was on Neosho— Neosho's story and Neosho's proposition to him earlier that day. He liked Neosho. Funny, he thought, at first he had disliked the man intensely, but now he liked him, and he sympathized with him, having heard the story of how Overton Avant's hired men had beat him up and caused him to lose his property. Of course, once the bank had foreclosed, Avant had purchased the mortgage.

But Neosho wanted Steele to join with him in a crusade to clean up West Riddle. He had seen him kill Alfalfa George, in spite of all Steele's imagined stealth, and had figured that maybe Steele was a man he could interest in the project. Neosho really had no plan, just a desire and a determination to do the job, but he needed help. He had sought out Steele for that help. Steele wasn't sure what he should do or what he wanted to do. Neosho had been done wrong and he deserved help in doing what could be done to right that wrong. But Steele wasn't sure that he was the man to supply that help. Yes, he had been playing gunfighter out in the woods alone, but he had never faced a man with a gun. He had killed two men, true enough, but he had killed the first with a knife and the second with a walking stick. Men who cleaned up tough towns were gunfighters. Besides, Steele thought, he needed to maintain a low profile. After all, as John Berringer Temple he was wanted for murder. He was in hiding. He was on the lam. No. That was an eastern expression. He was on the scout. He wished that he had never had that drink with Neosho. Then he wouldn't be worrying about these things. *Damn that smiling cowboy,* he thought.

He had his own problems. As J. B. Temple he was wanted in New York—perhaps everywhere. He really had no idea how widely Temple might be sought by the law. As Blue Steele he had fled the Cherokee Nation, and he certainly wouldn't be welcomed back to New Hampshire, and now, as Tyrone Hamlin, he had killed again, and he had been seen. Yes, he had his own problems. Why should he worry about the problems of some cowboy? The cowboy really didn't even have any problems. He could walk away from all this. Besides that, Steele thought, what about the problems of his own people, the Cherokees? If he were going to undertake a small war, shouldn't it be on behalf of the Cherokees against the United States? Of course, that would be pointless—a suicide mission. Then too, he wasn't really sure that he was Cherokee. His mother was a white woman. That meant that he had no clan. How could a man with no clan be Cherokee? But the federal government was beginning to determine the way in which the Cherokees kept their rolls, and Bluford Steele was on the roll as the son of Chickenhawk. He didn't know who his people were. He didn't know if he had any people. He felt very much alone in the world. The closest thing to home anymore, he thought, was Seagraves' acting company, and he was getting ready to leave that.

Of course, there was still the problem of Seagraves' money. Alfalfa George hadn't had that money on him when Steele had killed him, and the money that George did have, the money which Steele had taken off George's body and given to Seagraves, wasn't anywhere near the amount that Seagraves had lost. Steele wanted to get Seagraves' money back for him. He hadn't mentioned that to Neosho. It would have just made Neosho's argument that much stronger. Steele felt like things were closing in on him. It was time to leave Seagraves and Company. Time to move on. Seagraves' money was Seagraves' problem, not Steele's. Besides, the old man would probably make enough here in Riddle to get by with, and by the time his whole western tour was over and done with, he'd have made plenty of profits. He wouldn't even miss the West Riddle cash. Neosho's ranch, Seagraves' money, the beating Neosho had suffered, the man Steele had seen fly through the window of Blanch's saloon and the image of the fat man sitting beside Blanch at the play puffing on a cigar and sipping a drink, these images raced through Steele's mind.

But the gunfighting. Steele thought about the day in St. Joseph when he had seen his first gunfight—the man in the street crazy with anger and shouting threats and obscenities, firing wild. The calm man who came out of the office, the object of the threats, who stood still as the wild shots slapped around him. Steele recalled the way in which the calm man had drawn his pistol out of its holster and fired once—the way in which the loudmouthed, threatening man had jerked when hit in the head with that one shot. But most of all he recalled the image of the cool killer—the gunfighter. He thought of himself in that role—wondered if he could remain so calm in the face of gunfire. He thought about his many identities, his many roles. He wondered if he could add this one to his list.

Steele strapped on the rapier which he would use in the duel with Tybalt. He slid the thin-bladed sword halfway out of its scabbard, then snapped it back in place. By God, he thought. In order to play Shakespeare he had had to become an expert with the rapier. Could becoming expert with the pistol be any more of a challenge than that? He hardly thought so.

Steele played Mercutio that night with a new life. There was more sense in the witty cynicism, more bite in the sarcasm and more fire in the duel. He saw Neosho in the audience. The cowboy didn't seem to be smiling. He seemed genuinely studious, but what was he studying, Steele wondered. Shakespeare or Steele? After the encores Steele avoided Neosho. He hurried up to his room and got himself ready for bed. He was glad that he had some rye whiskey in his flask.

Steele slept late the following morning. He woke up a couple of times, but he wasn't at all anxious to show himself around town, so he stayed in bed and slept longer. When he could no longer sleep, he dragged himself out of bed and washed his face. He dressed himself slowly, took a swallow out of his flask, and as his stomach was growling, decided that he would have to go out into the town and find himself some breakfast. He went downstairs and left the hotel. He thought that he would have less chance of running into someone he knew if he found someplace else to eat. He remembered a little place down the street and around the corner, so he walked over to it, went inside and ordered himself a mess of scrambled eggs, some fried potatoes and bacon.

Steele had just finished his breakfast and was sitting alone drinking black coffee when Brice Seagraves came bursting through the door.

"There you are," said the old man. "I've been looking all over this town for you, Johnny."

Steele looked quickly around when he heard Seagraves call him by what the old actor thought was his real name. There was no one in the room but the greasy cook, and he didn't even look up from his work behind the counter. Steele figured it was all right.

"Now that you've found me," he said, "sit down and have some coffee with me, Brice."

"No thanks," said Seagraves. "I didn't come for coffee."

He sat down at the table with Steele tossing a folded newspaper on the table between them.

"It's the New York *Times,*" he said. "It came on the stage yesterday to Miller. When I saw it I asked him if I could take a look at it after he was finished. He gave it to me and told me to go ahead and read it. Said he was in no hurry for it. It's about a month old already."

Seagraves opened up the paper and tapped on a picture with his stubby finger.

"Here you are, Johnny," he said. "Right here."

There was a photograph of "John Berringer Temple" with his flowing hair and moustache. The caption read, "FAMOUS ACTOR DISAPPEARS AFTER STABBING INCIDENT."

"I'm glad they used that picture," said Steele. "It's always been my favorite. Was my performance reviewed?"

"Oh, hell, Johnny, I didn't look for any reviews. I didn't even read the blasted article. This is the first thing I saw. Someone might recognize you from that picture. Things are catching up to you, my boy."

"Um, yes," said Steele. "You're right, of course. I don't think that anyone will recognize me right away with my hair cut and whiskers shaved off, but it could happen. Especially if anyone has the intelligence to seek J. B. Temple among a troupe of traveling players. Has anyone else seen this paper?"

"No one that I know of," said Seagraves, "but I can't keep it forever. I'll have to return it to Miller."

"Yes. Keep it until tomorrow, will you? I'll play Macduff for you tonight, and then I'll take my leave. You should have time enough between now and your next engagement to restructure your plays."

"Yes. I can do that."

"Of course," Steele continued, "you never know who else out here in the wilds might have received a copy of the New York *Times.* It's probably rare, but you never can tell."

Steele quickly analyzed his situation. There didn't seem

to be many alternatives. With the story and picture of "Temple" circulating, an acting company no longer seemed a safe place to hide. He made up his mind.

"Have you seen that smiling cowboy around town this morning?" he said.

"What?" said Seagraves. "You mean that young fellow who accosted us yesterday morning over breakfast?"

"Yes. That's the one."

"Why yes. I believe I saw him in the saloon—the one in the hotel. He was drinking alone, I believe. What in the world do you want with him?"

"Never mind, Brice," said Steele. "And just forget that I asked, will you? Don't worry about anything."

Steele paid for his breakfast and left. He walked with Seagraves back to the hotel, and as they entered the front door, Steele gave the old man a pat on the shoulder.

"I'll see you later, Brice," he said, and he walked into the saloon.

"Howdy there, Mr. Hamlin."

Steele felt panic suddenly deep in his guts as he turned to face the booming voice that greeted him from the first table inside the door. It was the marshal, Bluff Luton, having a cup of coffee by himself. Steele stared in spite of himself at the big star on the man's chest. His heart pounded. What if the town marshal knew that Tyrone Hamlin was in fact John Berringer Temple, the escaped murderer from New York? He quickly composed himself.

"Good morning, Mr. Luton," he said.

"Call me Sarge," said Luton. "Everybody does."

"Yes," said Steele. "Well, uh, all right, Sarge. Excuse me."

Just as Seagraves had said, Neosho was seated alone at a table in the middle of the room. He had a bottle of rye whiskey in front of him on the table. Steele chuckled to himself and wondered whether or not the rye whiskey was there to attract him to the cowboy's company. He brushed

past Luton and headed toward the bar, making it a point
to pass by Neosho on the way. As he neared Neosho's table,
he paused.

"Hello, cowboy," he said in a loud voice.

"Why, good morning, Mr. Hamlin."

"Did I see you at the play last night?"

"Well, I don't know about that," said Neosho, "but I was
sure there. It was a hell of a good show, too."

"Thank you," said Steele. "I'm glad you enjoyed it."
Then he lowered his voice. "Meet me tonight," he said,
"behind the hotel, two hours after the play."

Steele walked on over to the bar and ordered a shot of
rye whiskey. As he downed it, he could see out of the
corner of his eye Sergeant Bluff Luton leave the hotel. He
headed back up the stairs towards his room, and upon
reaching the landing, turned and looked down at Neosho.
He touched the brim of his hat and headed for his room.

Alone at his table, Neosho scratched his head in puzzlement. He sensed that Steele had something to tell him or
something to do, and that he wanted to keep it on the sly.
Well, that was fine with him. He would be there.

Once again Steele sat alone in the dressing room prepar-
ing for the evening performance. Once again Steele's
thoughts were not on the coming performance. Tyrone
Hamlin would disappear that night. After his final appearance as Macduff in Riddle, Iowa, the traveling player
known as Tyrone Hamlin would never again be heard of.
His usefulness was over, and Blue Steele would kill him as
easily as he had killed Chester and Alfalfa George and John
B. Temple. More easily. Steele had on his beard and wig,
his kilt, his big broadsword and all of his makeup for the
part of Macduff, and it was still early. He carefully packed
up his makeup kit and stashed it in a corner of the room
out of the way. Beside it he placed his gunbelt and Chester's cane. Over all of that he tossed his street clothes,

including his big cloak. No one would bother any of it until he got back to it after the play. He took a shot of rye whiskey out of his flask, tucked the flask in under the cloak, then disappeared into the blackness of backstage to await the opening curtain.

Across the river in West Riddle the cowboy, Neosho, had just tied his horse to a rail on a dark back street. He didn't know what the actor, Hamlin, wanted with him—why he wanted him to be in the alley behind the theater that night after the play—two hours after the play. He didn't know what Hamlin had in mind, but it occurred to him that maybe Hamlin was going to agree to help him in his fight against West Riddle. He hoped so. If not, he asked himself, why had he been so secretive with him about the meeting? Neosho, too, knew that the actors would be leaving Riddle after tonight's performance. If Hamlin was going to join up with Neosho, then he would need a good horse.

Neosho walked the shadows and made his way to the back of the stable. Charlie Lewis, the man who owned the stable, so far as Neosho knew, was not an Avant man, and Neosho didn't want to hurt him. But he wanted an extra horse, and the horse that had belonged to Alfalfa George was a good one. A little fooling with the hasp on the back door, and Neosho had it opened. He slipped quietly inside. No one seemed to be around. He located the horse he wanted and found the saddle, too, thrown over the gate to the stall. Working quickly but quietly, he saddled up the horse, then laboriously penciled a note which he stuck prominently on a nail in the empty stall.

I figger that you probly owne this heer hors that is if Jorge owed you monie when he got hisself killed and I aint got nothin aginst you and dont want to do you no

rong so I just want you to no that youl git payed. I dont
no just when.

He thought about it for a moment, then signed his name.

Two hours after the final curtain of *Macbeth* in Riddle,
Neosho rode into the alley behind the hotel leading the
horse that had belonged to Alfalfa George. He sat for a
long moment uneasily in the saddle. Then Blue Steele
stepped out of the shadows.

"Hamlin?" said Neosho.

"It's me," said the actor.

"I brung you a horse."

"Then let's get out of here. We'll talk later."

The actor climbed onto the riderless horse holding his
clumsy bundle in one hand. He put his weight on his feet
in the stirrups, lifted himself slightly from the saddle and
threw his weight forward.

"Lead the way," he said.

Neosho squinted through the darkness at the strange
way the man sat a horse, but he figured that he should
keep his mouth shut, at least for the time being. He turned
his mount around.

"Follow me," he said.

He led the actor back to the Missouri River bridge and
across it, but just as they crossed into West Riddle, Neosho
took a hard turn north and rode out of town and out onto
the prairie. They rode north across treeless, flat prairies,
the hills and trees of the riverbank off to their right. They
rode most of the rest of the night before Neosho turned
back toward the river. The actor was exhausted from the
combination of his eastern riding style and the distance of
the ride. He followed Neosho into the trees and through a
winding path up into small hills to a low-slung, one-room
log cabin built back into the side of a hill. It's no wonder
Avant's men hadn't found it, he thought. Looking for it

even, one could ride right past it. They dismounted, and Neosho unsaddled the horses and turned them into a small corral just beside the cabin. Then he led the actor to the front door of the cabin, but as he reached for it, it opened from inside. A young girl stood in the doorway.

"Neosho," she said, and she threw her arms around the young cowboy's neck and kissed his lips. Neosho finally struggled to free himself from her embrace.

"Honey," he said, "I've brought someone home."

The girl let go of Neosho and backed into the cabin to let the men get through the doorway. Her cheeks flushed slightly.

"Maribel," said Neosho after he had closed the door behind them, "this here is . . ."

The actor, still toting his awkward bundle, didn't allow Neosho to finish his sentence.

"Abel Kane," he said, extending his hand.

The girl put her small hand in his. It was soft and smooth, and its touch thrilled the newly created Abel Kane. He bent to kiss it.

"Oh," she said.

"Uh, this here is my girl I told you about," said Neosho. "This is Maribel Carver."

"I'm pleased to meet you, Miss Carver."

"Pleased to meet you, Mr. Kane," said Maribel, running to the table and pulling out a chair. "Won't you sit down? I'll get some coffee."

"Abel Kane?" said Neosho, pulling out his own chair and joining the other at the table. "Where the hell did that come from?"

"One reason that I decided to join with you on this enterprise was that things seemed to be catching up with me. I had a need to start all over again. I needed a new identity—a new name. Tyrone Hamlin is gone forever. He never really existed anyway. I made him up, too. So my name is Abel Kane."

"Why Abel Kane?" said Neosho.

"Because I'm both the killer and the victim."

Neosho scratched his head in puzzlement while Maribel shot a worried look toward their visitor.

"You say you made up Mr. Hamlin?" said Neosho. "Then you ain't him either?"

"That's right."

"Well, then, just who the hell are you?"

Maribel, who had been listening intently to all this conversation, brought three cups of coffee to the table. The actor looked from Neosho to the girl.

"Oh, hell," said Neosho, "forget I said that. It ain't none of my business who you are. I had no call to go prying like that. I'm just glad that you're here."

The actor took a sip of his coffee. It was hot.

"I suppose," he said, "since you two are taking me into your home, I shouldn't worry about taking you into my confidence. My real name is John Berringer Temple. I'm a professional actor from New York City. At least I was. I had just reached the height of my profession. I was about to become recognized as the greatest star of the American theater, when I killed a man in a fight. I'm wanted for murder in New York."

A frightened expression flashed across Maribel's face.

"There's nothing for you to be afraid of. I'm not a murderer. Well, really I suppose I am, but I mean, I'm not a cold-blooded murderer. I'm not at all what I think of when I think of a murderer. The man I killed in New York was trying to thrash me with a walking stick."

Steele reached down into his bundle and withdrew the knurly cane.

"This one," he said. "If I hadn't killed him defending myself, he might very well have killed me with this thing. It's quite possible."

"I know," said Neosho.

"Oh, yes," said the actor, recalling that Neosho had witnessed his bludgeoning of Alfalfa George. "I have killed another man since then, but he had robbed my friend and employer—actually, when you get right down to it, he had robbed me and a number of other people as well. I—well —I suppose it was a cold-blooded murder."

Steele suddenly felt guilty for the first time. He looked quickly from Neosho to Maribel. He had never before tried to explain—to justify—what he had done to someone else. He found that it wasn't easy. It sounded much worse when put into words. He felt a fool. He should have kept quiet, he thought. He wondered why he had confided in them his previous identity of John B. Temple but not his real one of Bluford Steele. He had told them a half truth. Maybe he felt like J. B. Temple was his real identity. Maybe he no longer knew who he was.

"Perhaps I shouldn't be here at all," he said.

"The hell," said Neosho. "Right here is just where you belong. I brought you here, didn't I? It's my home—sort of. And didn't I see you give it to Alfalfa George? And ain't that exactly why I went and looked you up? Maybe that was a cold-blooded murder. I don't know. I ain't no lawyer. But if it was, then there wasn't never a man who deserved to be cold-blooded murdered more than he did."

"I know who that man was, Mr. Temple," said Maribel. "I know what he did to Neosho, too. I don't know anything about what you did in New York, but whatever you say is good enough for me. You're welcome here."

"Thank you both," said the actor. "But please, call me Abel."

"All right Abel," said Neosho, "and now that I've heard that story, I reckon I know where you learned how to ride a horse—Noo York. First thing after we've had a good sleep, we'll work on that."

CHAPTER SIX

Confronted by Neosho with his lack of riding skill, Blue Steele was suddenly pleased that he had concealed the whole truth of his identity from Neosho and Maribel. Never mind that the Cherokees were an eastern tribe of mountain-dwelling farmers and not a nation of horse people like the many Plains Indian tribes. He knew how white people thought about Indians, and he knew that Neosho, if apprised of the truth regarding Bluford Steele, would be amazed at an Indian who couldn't ride. It was all just as well.

"First thing, Abel," said Neosho, "that there saddle is made to set in. Set in it. Settle down. Scoot your butt back a little there. Hell, you might mash your nuts the way you're setting. There. That's more like it. Now, don't hold your back stiff like that. You don't need to set so prim and proper-like on a nag like that. Relax. Boy, you must a been plumb wore out after riding all that way last night."

"Yes, I was rather—uh, that is, you're right as rain, ole hoss. I was plumb tuckered out."

Steele slouched in the saddle. He was wearing range clothes given him by Neosho, and he had begun to let his beard grow—not so it looked like a beard, just to look unshaven. He had washed the grease out of his hair and left it dry. An unruly wave hung down on his forehead beneath the wide brim of the Stetson Neosho had crammed on his head. His six-gun hung at his side.

"All right," shouted Neosho. "Let's ride."

So the actor began to build another character—Abel

Kane. He was learning to ride like a westerner. He imitated the speech patterns and the diction of Neosho. He aped Neosho's ambling walk. He became absorbed in his new role.

Sitting in the shade in front of Neosho's cabin with fresh coffee Maribel had brought, after a long morning ride, Steele leaned back onto a tree.

"I think I'm beginning to get the hang of it," he said.

"Hell," said Neosho, "I'd say you are. You look like you was born to the range. No one would ever take you for no eastern dude. Not now."

Steele wondered to himself what Neosho would think and how he would react if Steele were to suddenly confide in him the truth of his identity.

"I have a good teacher," he said. "Let's do some shooting."

The two men walked to the far side of the cabin away from the corral. A rail fence ran away from the cabin along the base of the hillside. They lined up a row of cans and bottles on the fence posts, then they stepped back away from the fence.

"Now," said Neosho, and both men drew and began firing at the targets. One after another the cans flew from the posts and the bottles shattered. Both guns were emptied. Both men began reloading.

"I don't know," said Neosho. "I think you're about as good as me. Maybe better. I wouldn't want to be facing you. I don't know which one of us would be left standing up—if either one."

"That's just the thing," said Steele. "Shooting bottles and cans is one thing. Shooting at a man is another. I've never faced a target that shoots back."

Neosho looked around.

"Come here," he said.

He led the way back to the fence.

"Stand here."

Blue Steele stood against the fence with his back to it while Neosho found two cans on the ground and placed one on a rail on each side of Steele.

"You trust me?" he said.

"Yeah."

"Then just stand there. Don't move. Whatever happens, don't move."

Neosho walked back to the spot they had shot from before. He suddenly turned, drew his gun and fired two quick shots, knocking the cans off the rails. Steele flinched. He thought of the calm gunfighter in St. Joseph.

"Now," said Neosho, "you know what it feels like to get shot at."

He looked around himself again and spotted a tree stump off a short distance to his right.

"Toss me one of them cans," he said.

Steele picked up a can and threw it to Neosho. Neosho placed the can on the stump.

"Now put up another one back down yonder," he said.

Steele put a can on a fence post. Neosho stood by the stump and judged the distance. He looked down at Steele beside the post with the can on it.

"Stand over just a little," he said. "Now when you see me go for my gun, you go for yours. But shoot at the can, not at me."

Blue Steele's heart thumped inside his chest. He shifted his feet on the ground and flexed the fingers of his right hand. He thought again of the gunman in St. Joseph. He stared at Neosho. Then he saw something—a look, a movement. He couldn't quite define it, but it was a signal. Neosho was making his move. Steele ripped out his pistol and fired. The two blasts sounded like one. Both cans spun off their stands. Both men stood as if stunned for an instant. Then Neosho holstered his gun.

"You just killed me, old buddy," he said.

"How could you tell?" said Steele.

Neosho strolled over to the fence. Reaching into a pocket of his trousers, he withdrew a penknife.

"Let me see that hogleg of yours," he said.

Blue handed his pistol, butt first, to Neosho. Neosho took it and deftly carved two notches on the handle.

"What's that for?" asked Blue.

"Give you a bit of an edge," said Neosho. "It ain't exactly a lie. You have killed two men."

"But not with that."

"You don't have to say how you done it," said Neosho. "And anybody sees these here notches won't ask how you done it. He'll just automatically think you done it with this."

Neosho turned the pistol around and dropped it into Blue's holster.

"I got a job to do tonight," he said. "You want to go along?"

"What sort of job?" said Blue.

"We're running low on cow meat here. Old Avant has got somebody running cows on my spread here now. I been taking what I need from him when I need it. I need it right now."

"We're going out there and steal a cow?" said Blue.

"That's the general idea. Nothing to it. Unless some outrider happens along."

"Let's go," said Blue. "I need some action."

They saddled their horses and rode down out of the hills and onto the flat rangeland. Soon they had located a few head of cattle milling around beside a creek bed. Neosho snaked out his rope.

"Watch this now," he said, and he headed for a fat, young bull on the edge of the small herd.

Neosho had the bull by the horns and was bringing it along, all his attention absorbed in the task, when two riders seemed to appear out of nowhere. They hadn't seen Blue sitting on his horse at some distance, and they rode

down hard on Neosho. He didn't see them until it was too
late. The first rider reached out with a rifle in his right
hand and smacked Neosho alongside the head as he bar-
reled past him. Neosho reeled in the saddle. Blue spurred
his horse and headed for the fracas about the time the
second rider threw a loop around the stunned Neosho and
dragged him to the ground. Neosho landed with a heavy
thud in a cloud of dust. The young bull bawled and pulled
at the rope. The horse, now riderless, pulled back. The
rider with Neosho on the end of his rope began to ride and
drag the cowboy along behind him. His companion raced
to catch up with him. Blue quickly dismounted. It wasn't
too long a shot for his pistol if he made it fast before they
got much more distance between them and him. He held
the pistol out at arm's length and steadied his right wrist
with his left hand. He squeezed off a round. There was a
scream, and the rider with the rope tossed both hands in
the air and flipped backwards off his horse. The horse kept
running.

"Damn," said Blue out loud. He hadn't thought about
the riderless horse continuing to drag Neosho. The other
rider turned in his saddle. Blue fired a couple of shots in his
direction, and the rider, seeing his partner dead on the
ground and not knowing who was behind him or how
many, turned back around and raced away into the darkness. Blue climbed back into the saddle and hurried after
Neosho. He lashed at his mount. If he didn't catch up
quick, he thought, it would be too late. He would lose
them in the darkness. He spurred the horse viciously. Finally, he caught up with Neosho, bouncing along on the
rough terrain. He tried to reach into his pocket for his
knife so he could cut the rope. He couldn't manage to get
to it. He raced ahead, but it was no use. He couldn't catch
up with the wild-running horse. He was having trouble
keeping his own mount from running over Neosho as he
raced along beside the helpless man trying to catch up

with the runaway. He drew his six-gun and fired. The runaway stumbled. It tried to keep going. Blue then rode up beside it and fired a shot into the side of its head, and it crumbled to the ground. He dismounted and rushed back to Neosho. The cowboy was unconscious and caked with blood and dirt, but he was alive.

Blue straightened him out, removed the rope from him, then loaded him onto his saddle. He led the horse back to where the chase had started. Neosho's horse and the bull were still playing tug-of-war, and they hadn't gotten very far away. How the hell was he going to get ahold of that horse with it fighting that damn bull. He drew his pistol and shot the bull between the eyes. The bull froze, shuddered and collapsed in a heap, its sudden dead weight causing the horse to slow down its own antics, then to stand still. Blue cut the rope and climbed into the saddle. He rode back over to where Neosho waited, loaded onto Blue's own saddle, and picked up the trailing reins.

"Damn," he said. "Now I hope I can find my damn way back."

Benjamin Goree rode hard into West Riddle. He jumped from the saddle at the hitching rail in front of Blanch's saloon without bothering about the puffing and blowing horse, and he rushed inside and up the stairs. At the far end of the hall, he stopped, panting, and banged on the door. He heard muffled voices inside. He banged again on the door. When Blanch Storey opened the door, still tying the belt around the waist of her pink dressing gown, Goree practically shoved her aside in his haste to see Overton Avant. Avant was sitting in a large, overstuffed chair on the opposite side of the room. He was wearing a satin robe. His smooth, pink feet were bare. He was lighting a cigar. The bed beside him was rumpled.

"Someone's just killed Charlie Hall," puffed Goree.

"Slow down and tell me just exactly what happened,"

said Avant, blowing billows of smoke up from his cigar. "Get me a drink, Blanch."

Blanch moved over to a nearby table and poured a glass of pink champagne. She handed it to Avant who gulped it down and handed the glass back to her. She refilled it and gave it to him again.

"Me and Charlie was out on the range," said Goree. "You know, the place what used to belong to that Neosho. We was riding together, and we come across someone rustling himself up a beef."

"One beef?" said Avant.

"That's what it looked like. It didn't look like no big rustling operation. Looked like one man trying to get himself some beef to eat. Well, we rode down on him, and Charlie throwed a rope on him and commenced to dragging him. But then pretty soon, here comes up another one behind us and shoots Charlie right out of the saddle. I couldn't hardly see him, and I didn't know if he had more friends, so I lit out."

"Did you get a look at the other one? The one Charlie was dragging?"

"I ain't for sure, Mr. Avant," said Goree, "but I think it was Neosho."

"Neosho," said Avant. "Damn."

He stood up and began to pace the floor, his pink feet sinking in the plush carpet.

"Benjamin," he said, "you're in charge. Take some men out there. Find out for sure if it's Neosho. Find out who's with him, how many there are, and where they're staying at. I want them. Dead or alive, I want them."

"I'm in charge, Mr. Avant?"

"You heard me right, Benjamin. You get them, whoever they are, off of that place and out of there however you have to. You get them for me, and there'll be a nice bonus in it for you. You hear?"

"I hear you, Mr. Avant," said Goree, "and I'll get right on it. Right now."

Goree turned and rushed out of the room leaving the door ajar in his haste. Blanch closed the door behind him and latched it. She turned slowly back toward Avant, then walked around behind his chair. Reaching down, she put a hand on each of Avant's fat, pink cheeks as the front of her gown fell open.

By the time Goree and his gang got out to the site of the recent fight, what had been Charlie Hall was already fly-blown. The sight and smell made even some of the hard-cases a bit queasy. The bull had been butchered.

"Let's get on the trail of those goddamned rustlers," said Goree.

"What about poor ole Charlie, here?" said one of the six men Goree had rounded up, a tough named Osgood Jones, who went by the name of Chicken.

"Hell," said Goree, "Charlie's way to hell past caring."

"We can't just leave him here like that," said Chicken. "We oughta at least give him a decent burial. God damn it, if somebody guns me down out here, I don't want you leaving me lay out like that, for flies and wolves and buzzards or whatever."

"Goddamn prairie dogs," said Mike McKinney, a burly ex-railroad gandy-dancer.

"Prairie dogs don't eat people," said Goree.

"Goddamn prairie dog'll eat anything that's dead," said McKinney. "They eat their own buddies once they're dead."

"I wouldn't want no prairie dogs eating me," said Chicken.

Goree stamped his feet in the dusty prairie ground.

"We've got a job to do, God damn it," he said. "We didn't bring no shovels, anyway."

"We could cover him over with rocks," said Chicken.

"You see any rocks around here?"

Chicken looked around, and with a pout on his lips, kicked at the dirt.

"I guess not," he said.

"Besides," said Goree, "if we could put him under the ground, he'd just get ate by worms. Didn't you know that?"

"Well," Chicken drawled, not wanting to give up the argument, "at least what was left of him wouldn't be out in the open like this for just anybody who was passing by to look at. It's embarrassing. I wouldn't want nobody looking at me like that. It's—well—it's kinda like watching somebody take a dump. It oughta be private, you know?"

"Tell you what, Chicken," said Goree, "you can stay here and bury him. Anybody else wants to help you, they can stay, too. I don't care a damn. Me and the rest are going to look for trail."

Everyone mounted up except Chicken. He stood with his hat off staring at the wretched remains of Charlie Hall. He looked up pleadingly at the gang on horseback.

"Ain't nobody gonna help me?" he whined.

"What you gonna dig with?" said McKinney.

"Gentry?" said Chicken, a whine still in his voice.

The man called Gentry, who up until that moment hadn't said a word, looked coldly at Chicken.

"I ain't gonna touch that," he said. "His skin will probably come off on your hands if you touch it. Might get sick."

Chicken's eyes opened wide. He hadn't thought of that. He looked at the corpse and at Gentry.

"Well," he said, climbing into his saddle, "I guess it ain't no different getting ate by prairie dogs than by worms. I guess it don't matter too much."

They rode circle around the open prairie for most of the rest of the morning and never found any sign of a trail. Then they rode into the woods for a ways. Finally, tired, nerves frayed, hungry and irritable, they returned to West

Riddle where Goree had to report to Overton Avant that they had had no success. Avant, in a rage, ordered Goree to go back out the next day. Neosho was obviously trying to strike back at him over the land he had lost. Avant couldn't afford to let anyone strike back. His reign of terror depended on always dealing the last blow—on everyone in the region knowing that to buck Avant was to court disaster. Two of his men had been killed now, and no one had been punished. Someone had to die for it. Neosho, Avant decided, was the guilty one—in both cases. He would see to it that the word was spread that Neosho had killed Alfalfa George and Charlie Hall. Neosho had to die.

Blue Steele stood leaning on the fence of the small corral which stood beside Neosho's cabin in the woods. Inside, Maribel was nursing the battered cowboy. Neosho would survive, but it would be some time, Blue figured, before the two of them would be able to ride out together and tackle Avant's crew. At least there was plenty of food. After Blue had managed to find his way back to the cabin with the injured Neosho, and he and Maribel had cleaned Neosho up and doctored him and made him as comfortable as possible, they had gone back out on the prairie to the bull Blue had shot and butchered him. They had packed as much meat in bundles as they could load onto Neosho's horse as a pack animal and carry with them on their two mounts and brought it back to the cabin. Standing aimlessly at the fence, Blue Steele decided to go into West Riddle. He couldn't take the waiting around. He knew he couldn't fight the whole crowd by himself, but, he thought, he might be able to find out something. He knew that Neosho would like to come up with some evidence against Avant to justify his attack. When the whole thing was over with, Neosho would like to be able to get back his ranch—legally. He wanted to be able to settle down here with his Maribel and raise a bunch of cattle and little

Neoshos and Maribels. No one in West Riddle knew Kane, and no one, Blue was sure, would recognize in Abel Kane the man they had known briefly as Tyrone Hamlin. He walked over to the cabin door and knocked softly. Maribel opened the door.

"You don't have to knock, Abel," she said. "This is your home, too."

"Thank you, Maribel," said Blue, "but it ain't, you know. It's yours and Neosho's. I ain't got a home. How's he doing?"

"I can talk for myself, damn it," said Neosho in a strained voice from the bed. "I'm all right. Those bastards will have to do more than drag me on a rope to do me in."

"Is there anything I can do?" said Steele. "Anything you need?"

"Naw, hell," said Neosho. "All I can do is lay up here like a hurt wolf and nurse my wounds. Nothing to do until I can get up out of here."

"Not right now, Abel," said Maribel. "Thanks."

"Well," said Blue, "in that case, I'm going to take a little ride into town."

"What for?" said Neosho, raising himself up on an elbow. "It's too dangerous. Don't you try to do nothing by yourself."

"Calm down, cowboy," said Blue. "I'm not fixing to start a fight. Not today. But no one has ever seen or heard of Abel Kane except the two of you. I figure I'll just nose around a bit. See what I can find out. I might see or hear something that will help us. I'm doing no good just sitting around here. And don't worry about me not coming back. I'll be back."

With Abel Kane well on his way into West Riddle, and Neosho resting quietly, Maribel decided to go out into the woods to pick some berries. She wandered a ways off from the cabin, over the hill and down the other side toward the river.

Benjamin Goree and his six sidekicks were out on the prairie not far from the spot they had left the remains of Charlie Hall the day before. Goree was determined to find some sign of Neosho and whoever it was who was helping him. He didn't want to risk the wrath of Overton Avant again, and he wanted that bonus. He was also seemingly in line to inherit the position vacated by the killing of Alfalfa George. If he could get that, there would be plenty more bonuses in the future. He knew that, and he knew that the getting of that position would depend on the way he handled this Neosho business.

"All right," he said, "this is what we're going to do. We're going to all separate. Each one of us go and look for any sign we can find of them rustlers. Any damn thing. Fan out around this damn prairie. Some of you comb them hills. Can't two men have come out here and killed poor Charlie and butchered a bull and not left no sign. We just ain't looked hard enough yet. I mean look. If you spot anything suspicious, fire off three shots. Whenever we hear three shots, we'll all come a running and gather up right back here."

"Back at this putrid spot?" said Chicken.

"You know another landmark out here in this desolate place? You hear three shots, hustle right back here."

The riders scattered, some, according to Goree's instructions, fanning out onto the prairie, others beginning to skirt the edge of the woods. A tall, thin rider whose back bowed so much that he almost formed an ess-curve in his saddle, and therefore had been dubbed "Snake," was one who skirted the woods. Snake Perrine rode slowly, studying the ground carefully. His eyes were thin slits in his face. His mouth was a lipless gash. Below his nose and on his pointed chin grew long, curly whiskers, but there weren't enough of them to call a beard. His clothes were grimy and threadbare, but the six-shooter strapped to his left thigh was clean. Perrine rode a quarter of a mile along the edge of the woods. He stopped and stared at the ground for a moment, then headed his horse into the trees. He had found a winding trail through the thick brush. When he came across the little cabin snugged back into the side of a hill, it startled him. He thought that it would have been easy to pass it right by. There was a small corral to one side, and Snake saw two horses in the corral. He pondered the situation. He could ride right up there and bust into the cabin, but he didn't know who was inside. He didn't know how many might be in there. It might be Neosho and his partner, but it might be someone else. He could knock at the door or call out, but then if Neosho was the one inside, he might just shoot first. Besides, he wasn't at all sure that Goree would want him to kill Neosho, not until Goree had given the order. Goree had just said to fire three shots upon the discovery of anything suspicious. Perrine quietly turned his horse around and headed back down the trail to the edge of the prairie. When he was back out in the open once more, he slicked out his shiny revolver, raised it up over his head and popped off three rounds. Soon he was joined near the remains of Charlie Hall by the other six riders.

"Who fired them shots?" said Benjamin Goree.

"It was me," said Snake.

"Well, what for?"

"I found a little cabin up there in the woods. Two horses in a corral."

Blue Steele stepped through the front door of Blanch's saloon. He paused for a few seconds just inside the swinging doors and coldly surveyed the room. It was full. Blanch was behind the bar. Off to one side where Alfalfa George used to lurk and keep an eye on things, there were two hooligans—Avant's men, Blue thought. He had seen them

before, but he didn't know their names. He was surprised
not to see more of them hanging about. He decided to give
his disguise the supreme test, so he marched straight for
the bar to confront Blanch.

"Lady," he said.

Blanch turned around to face the customer.

"How about a shot of rye whiskey?" he said.

"Sure thing, stranger," said Blanch. She shoved a shot
glass toward Blue and bent over to withdraw a bottle from
underneath the bar. She poured the drink.

"Leave the bottle," said Blue. He tossed down the first
drink and poured himself a second.

"You're new in town, aren't you?" said Blanch.

"Yep."

"Just passing through?"

"You never know," said Blue. Out of the corner of his
eye, he thought he could see Avant's hooligans giving the
stare. He finished his second drink and poured a third.
Turning his back on Blanch, he leaned his elbows on the
bar and faced out into the room. He glanced toward the
hooligans, and they quickly averted their eyes. Too obvious, he thought. Now that he was here, what was he going
to do? He wasn't sure. It had seemed like a good idea
earlier, before he had left the cabin. He would test his
disguise—well, he had tested it. It was good. He had
known it would be, though, so really, if that had been the
whole purpose of his trip to town, it had been a waste. As
J. B. Temple, Blue Steele had become an expert with
makeup, and although a disguise calls for some different
techniques than does stage makeup, he could easily alter
his techniques to fit the purpose. So what was he doing
here? He had thought that he might find out something.
But what? What Avant and his cronies were up to? Some
kind of incriminating evidence against Avant? He still
wanted to get Brice Seagraves' money back for him, too.
But how was posing against the bar in this saloon going to

help accomplish any of that? He didn't know. Then he had a thought. He turned back around.

"Hey, lady," he called.

Blanch was at the far end of the bar pouring someone a drink.

"What do you want, stranger?" said Blanch, hardly looking back in his direction. But the stranger didn't answer, so Blanch straightened up and gave him a direct look. He jerked his head to indicate that he wanted her to come to him. Blanch stuck her hands on her hips in an exaggerated expression of impatience and walked down the bar to where Blue waited.

"Well, what is it?" she said.

"I'm looking for someone. Thought maybe you could help me."

"Yeah? Well, who you looking for? Anyone in particular?"

"Yeah. A cowboy name of Neosho. Leastwise, that's what he was going by when I last seen him."

"What do you want with this Neosho?"

"That's my business. Do you know him?"

"No. He used to live around here. Couple of years ago. I haven't seen him since."

"I heard that he was headed back this way."

Then a third voice intruded itself into the conversation.

"What's going on here, Blanch?"

It was one of the hooligans who had been standing against the wall. He had slipped up beside Blue and was leaning on the bar. His buddy was standing back of him a couple of steps.

"This ain't your conversation, mister," said Blue.

"It is now."

Blue turned so that only his left elbow rested on the bar. He was facing the newcomers, his right hand free. The one doing the talking looked down at the six-gun at Blue's side. He saw three notches.

"Maybe I can help," he said.

"Maybe."

"Well, then, relax, stranger. Let me buy you a drink."

Blue looked at the second thug, still standing away from the bar.

"You want me to turn back around to the bar and fill my right hand with a shot glass while shitface, here, is standing behind me?"

"You sonofabitch," snarled the shitface, slapping wildly at his holster.

Blue Steele's notched six-shooter was out, the cold barrel touching shitface under the chin before he could even clear leather. He froze, his jaw hanging down, eyes opened wide, afraid to blink.

"Take it easy," said the man at the bar. "We'll go sit at a table, all right? Wherever you like. I'm Cutter Macklin, and this here—shitface—is Slick Poppen. Come on. Maybe we can help you out."

"You lead the way," said Blue. "Both of you."

Macklin and Poppen started to walk toward a table.

"Wait a minute," said Blue. "Take the bottle. And the glasses. Get that table over there and leave me the seat to the wall."

Macklin picked up the bottle and told Poppen to get the glasses, then led the way to the table designated by Blue. Blue followed and sat down with his back to the wall. He stared hard at Cutter Macklin.

"Well," said Cutter, stammering a bit, "you got us at a disadvantage, stranger. You know who we are. Uh, what's your handle?"

"I'm Abel Kane."

"You're, uh, new to these parts, ain't you?"

"I'm looking for a cowboy called Neosho."

"I know Neosho," said Cutter. "Mind if I ask what you want with him?"

"That's my business."

"I'm trying to be friendly, Kane," said Cutter. "Could be, if I knowed why you want to find this Neosho, I might be able to tell you where to look. He used to have a little spread just outside of town here."

"Has he been around lately?"

"Yep."

Blue Steele reached for the bottle of rye and poured himself a drink.

"I'm going to kill the little bastard," he said.

Benjamin Goree dismounted and motioned the others to do likewise. He squatted in the prairie dust, shoving his hat back on his head.

"Was anybody in that cabin, do you reckon, Snake?" he said.

Snake squatted down beside Goree.

"I didn't get up too close," he said, "but there's a little corral beside it, and they was two horses in there."

"Just two horses?"

"Just two."

"Well," said Goree, "I bet someone's in there. We know that Neosho's hiding around here somewheres, and this here used to be his spread. We didn't even know that place was in there, so it's likely that that's him in there."

"Him or his buddy that's with him," said Mike McKinney.

"That's right," said Goree. "There's two of them. And there's two horses in there, so likely they're both of them to home. Now, they ain't got nothing nor don't know nothing that we need. All we got to do is to just kill them. They killed Alfalfa and they killed Charlie. So let's go in there and get the sonofabitches. Come on."

Goree climbed back into his saddle. He was proud of his little speech, and he was thinking of his coming bonus. He hoped that Neosho was in the cabin.

"Lead the way, Snake," he shouted.

Snake headed back for the trail into the woods. Goree turned in his saddle and called back to the last two riders.

"Simp," he said, "you and Gurnsey stay back here and watch the trail in case anyone else comes riding by. If you see strangers, don't ask no questions. Just shoot."

The five riders led by Snake Perrine picked their way slowly along the wooded trail until they arrived close to the cabin. Snake halted them and pointed out the snug hiding place of the tiny abode. Goree scratched his face, deciding what to do next.

"Get down off your horses," he said, "and keep quiet."

The men dismounted and tied their animals to trees. Each drew out his pistol except Chicken who drew a sawed-off shotgun from a special saddle holster.

"Now," said Goree, "they's probably only two men in there, but we ain't sure, and even if that's right, they ain't no sense in any of us getting shot. So let's just ease ourselfs on up to that cabin real slow and quiet. Let's go."

Leading the way, Goree took himself to the front door of the cabin. He motioned Chicken to come up with him on the other side of the door. Snake stood about six paces away directly facing the door. Gentry lurked by the window, and McKinney was alongside the wall on the other side of the door. Goree looked from one side to the other, checking the position of his men, still motioning for quiet. He raised his pistol and thumbed back the hammer. Chicken cocked the two shotgun hammers. Other clicks could be heard around the small cabin.

Inside, Neosho had been lying in a half sleep. He had been longing for Maribel, remembering the feel of her soft flesh against his. He wished that he had been more careful the night he went looking for beef. His bruised and scabby body was causing him all kinds of problems. It was keeping him from riding with Abel Kane and getting started with their job. And it was keeping him from making love with Maribel. Those were the two most important things in his life—and the two most important people in his life. He wondered about Abel Kane or Tyrone Hamlin or J. B. Temple, or whoever the man was. What kind of man was he? An actor. An actor turned gunfighter, and a hell of a gunfighter he was going to make, too, Neosho thought. He was a strange one, a hard man to get close to, yet a man who inspired confidence. Neosho felt that he could trust Abel Kane. He could trust him with his life. He could leave him alone with Maribel and not be worried. He didn't feel like he really knew the man, but he felt like he could call him friend.

While he was thus caught up in his reverie, Neosho suddenly was startled by a noise from outside. It was a slight noise and undefinable, and it might have been nothing, but he didn't want to take any chances. He struggled up on his left elbow and reached painfully for the six-gun in the holster hanging from the back of a chair near his bed. He drew it out and cocked it, watching the door.

Outside, Benjamin Goree reared back and lifted his huge foot in the air, then, with a mighty effort, kicked all his weight against the door. The door gave way easily to the force of Goree's thrust, and his weight and forward motion carried him right on through into the cabin. Neosho fired. His bullet tore away the right cheek from Goree's face. Goree spun wildly, slinging blood onto the face of Chicken, who came scurrying past him into the cabin. Quickly taking in the situation, Chicken jabbed the barrels of his short shotgun at Neosho and pulled the triggers. The blast was deafening inside the small cabin, and the shot splattered into the bare chest of Neosho, causing his shoulders and head to slump down grotesquely toward the lower part of his body. He was dead instantly, his blood soaking into the bedclothes, running down onto the floor from splotches on the wall behind him.

"Oh, oh, God damn," said Chicken, a horror-stricken look on his face. He was looking at Goree while wiping

Goree's blood from his own face. Goree cringed in the doorway making rasping noises from deep down in his throat. He was feeling his face with both hands. His eyes were wide, and there was no color left to his skin. Snake stepped to the door, looked at Goree calmly, then at Chicken.

"Who was in there?" he said.

"Oh, damn," said Chicken, wiping his face with his sleeve. "God damn."

Snake stepped over the writhing Goree and walked into the room. He went straight to the bed. Taking the body by the hair of the head, he lifted it to see the face.

"Neosho," he said, letting it drop back down. "Let's go back to town."

As Snake stepped back outside and headed back toward the horses, McKinney stepped toward the door.

"What's happened to Ben?" he said.

Chicken scampered over Goree and outside.

"His goddamn face is shot off," he said, and he ran for his horse where he quickly holstered the shotgun, then gingerly pulled off his shirt, tossing it into the bushes. "Euh," he said. "Damn."

"Hey," shouted McKinney, "what are we going to do about Ben?"

"Help him up on his horse, I guess," said Gentry. "We can't do nothing for him here. Got to get back to town."

"Well, bring me his horse," said McKinney, and he went to Goree, taking him by the arm and helping him to his feet. Gentry trotted over to the horses, mounted his and led Goree's down to the cabin. Snake was sitting on his mount, waiting calmly for the others to get ready. Chicken had mounted up and he rode slowly back down to the cabin. McKinney struggled to get Goree into the saddle, then climbed into his own.

"You reckon he'll make it back to town?" said Gentry.

"Probably bleed to death," said McKinney.

"We oughta do something," said Gentry.

Chicken was dropping new shells into his gun.

"We ain't no doctors," said McKinney. "What can we do? All we can do is get on back to town as fast as we can. Maybe we'll get there in time."

Gasping noises came from the throat of Benjamin Goree.

"It ain't human to let a man suffer like that," said Chicken, as he raised the double-barreled gun and leveled it at Goree's chest.

Goree's gasps became louder and more frantic.

"It's almost as bad as leaving a man's body to rot out on the prairie."

Chicken pulled the trigger, and the rest of Goree's face was ripped away as his body was flung backward out of the saddle by the blast of the shotgun. Chicken reloaded and holstered the gun.

"We gonna bury him?" asked McKinney.

"Hell, no," said Chicken, turning his horse to head for the trail back to town.

Cutter Macklin was in the plush room at the end of the hallway upstairs in Blanch's saloon. He was standing a few steps inside the doorway, his hat in his hands, facing Overton Avant who was squashed comfortably in the overstuffed chair. Avant puffed a cigar. He had a glass of champagne in his pudgy fingers.

"Said his name was Abel Kane," said Macklin. "Said he was looking for Neosho. He wants to kill the little bastard, he said."

"Did he say why he wants to kill Neosho?" said Avant.

"Well, he did after I kept asking him several times. He said that he had a sister and that Neosho had run off with her. So he's going to kill him."

"What kind of a man is he, do you think?" said Avant, then added with a chuckle, "A moralist?"

"I don't know about that, but he's a tough one. He's got three notches on his gun, and he's fast with it. Slick drawed on him, and this here Kane had his gun out and cocked and under Slick's chin before Slick could even get his out. And Slick drawed first. He's fast."

"Why did Slick draw on this Kane?"

"Well, sir, because Kane called him 'shitface,' " said Macklin.

Avant laughed a loud, shrill laugh, and when it died down, turned down his champagne glass and set it aside. He puffed on his cigar.

"I'll be down to see him directly, Cutter," he said. "Keep him here. Stay with him. I'll be right down."

"Yes sir," said Macklin, backing toward the door with a kind of an awkward shuffle. "I'll keep him down there for you."

Macklin left the room, and Avant heaved himself up out of the chair and found his coat. He went to the mirror on the wall and began to primp and straighten himself up to meet Abel Kane. He sounded like an interesting man, and more, one who shared an interest with him—the death of Neosho. Perhaps they could help each other out. Perhaps this Abel Kane would be looking for a job. Avant could use a man like that. Cold, calculating and fast with a gun. He might even replace Alfalfa George. None of the others could, really. Certainly not that stupid Goree. Goree wanted the job, Avant knew. But Goree wasn't fit for it. Now this Abel Kane—he sounded very interesting.

Avant slicked back his hair and left the room. He walked down the long hallway and turned down the staircase. About halfway down, he could see Cutter Macklin and Slick Poppen sitting at a table, and with them—Abel Kane, he thought. Even from this distance, thought Avant, he could see the hardness in the man. He wanted him. He needed him. A man like that could whip the whole territory into shape. But he would have to be careful how he

approached this man. He couldn't let him know how much
he wanted him—that he needed him. A man like that
could be dangerous if he knew his own worth. Avant
reached the bottom of the stairs and crossed the room to
Macklin.

"Cutter," he said.

Macklin jumped up from his chair, followed, a little
slowly, by Slick Poppen. Blue Steele sat still, watching the
other three men with a cold look. Avant liked that look.

"Mr. Avant," said Macklin, "this here is Abel Kane, the
man I was telling you about."

"Mr. Kane," said Avant, smiling and extending his hand,
"I'm Overton Avant."

Blue nodded. He did not accept the offered hand. Avant
looked at Macklin and Poppen.

"Beat it, boys," he said. "Mind if I sit down?"

"Suit yourself," said Blue.

Avant sat down. Blanch came hurrying over to the table
with a bottle of champagne. Blue Steele poured himself a
shot of rye whiskey and downed it.

"What do you want?" he said.

"I'd like to talk business," said Avant.

"What kind of business you in?"

"Any kind that makes money. Right now I want to talk
about a man called Neosho. I understand you're looking
for him."

"You know that I want to kill him," said Blue. "Your
lapdog ran up and told you that. Let's don't beat around
the bush. What do you want?"

"I want the man dead, too. I'll pay you to kill him, just so
I know it's done and to get it done quick. What's more, I
want to offer you a steady job when that's done."

"Doing what?"

"The same kind of work," said Avant. "And herding this
bunch of idiots I have working for me. I need them to

maintain some kind of control around here, but I need someone like you to control them. What do you say?"

"I'm going to kill Neosho anyway," said Blue. "I'll do that, and then I'll come back and talk to you again. We'll see."

"That's fair enough, Mr. Kane," said Avant, once more extending his hand. "Will you shake on that now?"

"Maybe when I come back," said Blue. "Be seeing you."

Blue got up and left the saloon, leaving Overton Avant standing alone at the table with his pudgy hand out in front of him. *So,* thought Blue, *now I can get in with Avant.* Maybe that would be a way to find the evidence that Neosho wanted. If it weren't for the fact that Neosho wanted his little place back legally, Blue thought, he would just kill that fat, disgusting Avant. He wouldn't have liked Avant even if he had not known about his evil activities. He was a sorry excuse for a human being. A thing like that, he thought, didn't deserve to live. Out on the sidewalk, Blue slowed down. He had made a beginning, but he still had no information with which to help Neosho's cause, and he was no closer to Seagraves' money. He glanced through the big window on the front of Blanch's saloon, and he could see Avant sitting down at the table to nurse his champagne, and probably his bruised ego. Blanch was still behind the bar.

Blue had spent enough time at Blanch's saloon as Tyrone Hamlin to know the layout pretty well. He didn't yet feel like going back to Neosho. He hadn't really accomplished anything. He had a quick idea. As Tyrone Hamlin, he had seen Avant going and coming occasionally from a room upstairs. Perhaps he lived there on a permanent basis. He walked around to the alley behind the saloon. On the back of the building was a stairway leading to a small landing with an outside door to the hallway on the second floor. He checked the alley and found no one around. Climbing the stairs quickly, he opened the door and looked inside. The hallway was empty. He went in and stepped to Avant's door. The door was locked.

"Damn," said Blue Steele.

As the room was the last one at the end of the hall, Blue thought it might have an outside window there by the landing. He went back out onto the landing. He was right. There, off to his right, was the window, but it would be quite a stretch to reach it from the landing. Blue glanced down the alley again in both directions. Still no one in sight. He leaned against the waist-high rail of the landing, and staying tight against the wall, reached with his right hand for the window. His left foot came up off the boards. His right hand found the edge of the window frame. The window was closed, so Blue had to ease his hand over to the top of the window casing. It was not locked, and Blue managed to press it upward a little at a time with his fingers. He was stretched out as far as he could go, his weight almost all on the rail around the landing. He had managed to get his left hand over against the window frame to hold some of his weight and to give him some balance while he was easing the window up with the fingers of his right hand. He had managed to raise the window about a foot, when the rail suddenly gave way under his weight. Blue's body swung out in an arc. He grabbed for the windowsill with his right hand, and as his body thudded against the wall, he slipped his left hand down to the sill. He was hanging at arm's length from the windowsill. He thought that this would be a hell of a fix for him to be in if someone happened down the alley. He pulled with his arms and scrambled with his feet against the side of the building, finally working his way up until he could poke his head in through the window. Happily, the room was empty, but he had expected it to be. He struggled the rest of the way through the window and onto the floor of Avant's pink room. He lay there on the floor for a moment, catching his breath. Then he sat up and looked around the room.

Just opposite the window was a desk. A likely place to start, thought Blue. He got up and went to the desk, jerking open the center drawer. He found a stack of bills which he stuffed into his own pocket. There were some letters, including one from Brice Seagraves agreeing to perform two shows, *Romeo and Juliet* and *Macbeth*, in West Riddle. Nothing particularly interesting. Nothing useful. Blue opened another drawer. There was a two-shot derringer, loaded. He smirked and shut the drawer, opening a third. It was filled with various kinds of legal papers. Blue took the stack of documents from the drawer and began thumbing through them. He could recognize that the majority of them were deeds and various kinds of property conveyances. Perhaps he would find the deed to Neosho's ranch, he thought. Then quickly he wondered if he would even know it if he came across it. It would have to have a name on it, something other than Neosho. And Neosho was all he knew. Besides, what legal validity had a stolen deed? Once again, Blue wondered what he was doing. Why had he come into town, and why had he broken into Avant's room? What did he think all of this was going to accomplish? As he quickly flipped through the papers, something caught his attention. He stopped and thumbed back three sheets.

"By God, it is here," he said aloud, but in a muted voice.

He held in his hand a deed. The phrase that caught his eye read, ". . . for the old Landsman place, lately owned by Ogden Vance of Texas, also known as Neosho . . ." Blue folded the deed and stuffed it into his shirt pocket. He flipped rapidly through the remaining documents, found nothing of immediate interest, and replaced the pile in the drawer. He opened the remaining drawers and looked inside them, but to no avail. He stood up and looked around the room. Nothing else seemed promising. He walked to the closet and opened the door. There on the floor of the closet stood a safe. Brice's money, he thought. But he didn't know how to open a safe without its combination. He was puzzling over this new dilemma, when he heard footsteps in the hallway. He quickly stepped partly into the closet and pulled the door after him, drawing out his six-gun at the same time. He waited. He could hear the sound of a key being inserted into the keyhole of the door, and he watched as the knob turned and the door was pushed into the room.

Blanch stepped inside and closed the door behind her. Her back was toward blue. He stepped out into the room, pointing the pistol at Blanch. He spoke softly.

"Go ahead and lock it," he said.

Blanch turned quickly with a loud gasp.

"Don't make any noise either," said Blue.

Blanch locked the door. She caught her breath and regained her composure.

"You," she said. "Abel Kane is it? What are you doing in here?"

"I might ask you the same question," said Blue. "I understand that you own this place, but it sure looks to me like Avant is running things. And this here is his room, ain't it? How come you've got a key to it and come up here alone?"

"I do own this place," Blanch said. "Mr. Avant rents this room from me. I came up here to . . ."

"Never mind," said Blue, cutting her off. "You'd just tell me a lie anyway."

He slowly drew back the hammer on his six-gun, the double-action clicks making an ominous sound in the stillness. Blanch's face whitened, even under her thick makeup.

"You're not going to shoot me?" she said. "Don't. Please don't. I'll do anything you say. I won't tell anyone I saw you here. Don't kill me."

"Can you open that safe?" said Blue.

Blanch hesitated a moment too long before answering. "No," she said.

"I think you're lying to me," said Blue.

"Why, I, uh . . ."

"Can you open it?" snapped Blue.

"Yes."

"Do it."

Blanch moved quickly and nervously to the safe on the closet floor. She knelt on the floor before it and began to work on the combination. Her hands were shaking, and it took her a bit longer than it ordinarily would have, but she got it opened, then turned to Blue with a questioning look on her face.

"Empty it out on the floor," he said.

Blanch pulled out the contents of the safe onto the floor there before her.

"Now," said Blue, "move right over there by the bed."

There on the floor was Brice Seagraves' cashbox. There was also loose cash, and there were more legal papers. Blue put the loose cash into his pockets, picked up the cashbox and opened it. It appeared to him that Avant hadn't even removed the cash. He had just stashed away the box intact. The fat sonofabitch, he thought. He tucked the cashbox under his arm, then moved to the window to look out into the alley. A wagon and team had been driven into the alley and stopped. There was a man on foot standing beside the wagon talking to the driver.

"Damn," said Blue. He didn't want to be seen leaving Blanch's place by the second-floor alley exit. Even with the deed, he wasn't sure how he was going to get Neosho's ranch back for him. Except for the finding of Seagraves' cash, the trip into West Riddle seemed to be a bust. And he wasn't yet out of town with the cashbox. He had to do something. He didn't want to wait around in the room he had just robbed either, and unless he killed Blanch, the usefulness of the new Abel Kane disguise had come to an abrupt end. The decision to come into town had been a hasty one, made out of boredom, and thought Blue, it had been a mistake. He didn't at all want to murder the woman. She was probably in cahoots with Avant. That much seemed to be more and more apparent. Still the idea of killing a woman was repugnant to Blue Steele. He remembered that there had been a Cherokee man who lived not far from where he had lived with his father, Chickenhawk, when he was a child. The man's name was Womankiller. Blue had never liked that man. He again looked out the window into the alley. The man who had been standing beside the wagon was climbing up onto the wagon seat beside the driver. Blue watched as the driver snapped the reins and the wagon lurched, then began to move slowly down the alley. He turned toward Blanch, the gun still in his hand.

"When I'm gone," he said, "you're going to tell Avant about me."

"No," she said. "I won't say anything."

She looked at the gun barrel which was pointed casually at her middle, and she trembled with fear.

"Don't shoot me," she said, her voice quavering.

"If I find out that you've said anything," said Blue, walking up close to Blanch, "I'll kill you. I'll come back in here in the middle of the night, and I'll cut your throat. Do you hear me?"

"Yes."

"Do you believe me? I'll do it."

Blue was lying, but he had to do something and get out of West Riddle. He thought that if he frightened Blanch badly enough, she might keep quiet at least long enough to allow him to get out of town and safely away.

"I won't say anything," she said. "I believe you."

Blue touched Blanch's neck with his gun barrel.

"Walk to the bed," he said.

Blanch walked stiffly to the edge of the bed. She held her head up high and looked down at the gun.

"Now," said Blue, "get down on the floor."

Blanch knelt beside the bed.

"Clear down," said Blue. "On your belly."

Blanch flattened herself against the floor, her face almost lost in Avant's plush pink carpet.

"Now crawl under the bed," said Blue. "Go on."

Blanch awkwardly inched herself forward until she was all the way under the brass bed. She could feel the sweat running down her face and dripping off onto the carpet pile.

"That's good," said Blue. "Now you stay there and keep quiet for fifteen minutes. When fifteen minutes has gone by, I'll be long gone and you can come out."

"I don't have a watch," said Blanch in a feeble voice.

"Count to sixty fifteen times," said Blue. "And count slow."

Blanch began counting in a low, quavering voice. Blue, Seagraves' cashbox under his arm, quietly left the room, shutting the door behind him. He went out into the alley by way of the landing door and stairway. Then he made his way back to his horse without encountering anyone. He rode for Neosho's cabin. Now that they had the deed, they could begin to make real plans for restoring Neosho's land to him. He wondered what Neosho would think of his having found his way into Avant's employ with a claim of having a desire to kill Neosho. Of course, that plan would have to be scrapped now that Blanch had seen him robbing Avant's room. She was probably telling Avant right now that he had been robbed by Abel Kane—that is, if she had come up yet with the courage to crawl out from under the bed. He heard a thundering of hooves ahead of him on the road, and he quickly rode into the thicket off to his right.

From his place of concealment, Blue Steele watched six

riders heading back toward town. He recognized a couple of them, though he didn't know them by name. They were Avant's men. He didn't panic, for he knew that Avant's men had been searching for signs around the site of the fight out on the prairie, but he did begin to worry a bit. He was suddenly anxious to get back to the cabin and make sure that everything was all right. When the riders were well past him on their way, Blue hurried his mount on toward the cabin.

CHAPTER SEVEN

It was dark by the time Blue reached the end of the wooded trail, and he saw that there was no light coming from the cabin. Perhaps with Blue gone, he thought, they were just being cautious. He rode slowly and as quietly as possible up to the little corral and tied his horse to the rail. Then he walked to the cabin door. He tapped lightly. There was no answer. Suddenly Blue was afraid, not for his own safety, but he felt a cold fear.

"Neosho," he said.

Still no one answered.

"Neosho. Maribel."

He opened the door, but he couldn't see in the darkness.

"Neosho," he said. "You in here? Maribel?"

He stepped gingerly into the dark room and reached into his pocket for a match. Then a voice came out of the darkness. It was Maribel's voice, and it was faint and feeble, but the suddenness of it startled Blue.

"That you, Abel?"

"Yes," he said, and he struck the match against the door. In the sudden flash of light, he saw the body of Neosho on the bed. He saw the blood. And he saw Maribel kneeling beside the bed, a blank, stunned expression on her face.

"Oh no," he said. "Oh, Maribel."

He rushed to the table to light the oil lamp, then took the lamp over to the bed and held it up, flooding light over the grisly scene. Neosho was dead. Someone had come while he was in town. Neosho had been murdered while he had been wasting his time in West Riddle. *God damn,* he thought. *Damn it. Damn me. Damn me for a fool.* The six men who had passed him on the road—they had to be the killers. He set the lamp down on a chair which stood nearby, and he put a hand on Maribel's shoulder.

"What happened?" he said.

"I was away," she said, her voice betraying no emotion. She spoke as if she were in a daze, as if she were in shock.

"I was out picking berries. I was going to make him a pie. I don't know what happened. I come home with my berries, and I found a dead man outside. He didn't have no face. He looked awful and it scared me. I dropped my berries out in the yard, and I come running in here. I found him. He's dead. I been sitting here ever since."

"Oh, Maribel," said Blue, "I should have been here. I shouldn't have gone to town. He told me not to go, but I was restless. I should have listened to him."

Maribel seemed to come out of her stupor somewhat. She turned her face to Blue. He noticed that her face was not streaked with tears. It just had a tired, listless, sad and very faraway look to it. She put her hand on his knee.

"It wasn't your fault, Abel," she said. "I wasn't here either. It wasn't nobody's fault. Except for them that done it."

Feelings of guilt and of responsibility overwhelmed Blue Steele. Neosho had depended on him. Now, he felt, Maribel depended on him. She might not say it. She might say that he had no further responsibility here, but Blue felt it. She needed him. Neosho would have said it.

"I'll get them, Maribel. I promise that."

"It don't matter. Nothing matters now."

Blue Steele leaned over the bed. He put a hand on each side of the dead Neosho's head and looked into its expressionless eyes.

"It matters to me," he said. "I'll get them. I'll get every last one of the scummy bastards, Neosho, every last one,

including that sybaritic swine, Overton Avant. I promise
you."

The next morning Blue Steele buried Neosho. He dug a
deep grave, and he piled rocks on top after he had put
back the earth. He placed a marker on top. It was a plain
wooden cross, and into the wood, Blue Steele had carved
an inscription:

NEOSHO
Murdered by Scum.
He was a man.
Take him for all in all,
I shall not look upon his like again.

Blue also saw the body of Goree for the first time. He
had missed it in the dark the night before. Maribel had
told him about finding the body, but he had not seen it.
Well, Neosho, he thought, *you got one of them anyhow. I'll
finish the job for you.*

Maribel fixed breakfast, and they ate in silence. She
refilled Blue's coffee cup.

"Maribel," he said, "I got the deed to this place. I was
going to give it to him. I guess I'll give it to you now."

"I don't want it," she said. "Not without him."

"You should have it. Even if you don't want to live here,
he'd want you to have the place. You could sell it once I get
it all legal and proper. The money would help you to settle
someplace else."

Maribel didn't answer, and Blue took the deed from his
pocket and held it out toward her. She sighed, took the
deed, got up from the table and walked over to the stove.
She opened up the firebox and pitched the document into
the fire. Blue felt as if she had smacked him in the face.
The deed was the only thing he had to justify his absence
to Maribel. Seagraves' money would mean nothing to her.

"All right, Maribel," said Blue, "what are you going to
do?"

"I don't know," she said. "I've got no place to go. Not now."

"I've got some things to take care of here," said Blue. "I want you to wait for me across the river where it's safe. Will you do that?"

"I ain't got no place to stay over there. I don't know nobody over there."

"I know some people over there. I'll take you and get you a place to stay. You just wait for me. Now why don't you pack up your things?"

"I don't have nothing in here that I want to take with me, Abel. Not now."

"You'll at least need some clothes," he answered. "Come on."

They pulled Maribel's few clothes together, and Blue tied them in a bundle. He got out his own bundle and lashed both bundles to Neosho's horse.

"Are you ready?" he said.

Maribel turned to look back at the cabin one more time.

"Burn it," she said.

"What?"

"Burn it down. Burn it down to the ground."

Blue went back inside. He fetched a stick from the firebox of the stove and touched it to the cloth cover on the table, then to the curtain on the one small window. Nothing else looked as if it would blaze up quickly, so he tossed the small torch onto the bed. He looked around, kicked a leg off the table in order to get himself a bar. He wedged the table leg in between the stove and the wall and pulled, toppling the stove and spilling the fire out onto the floor. He left the cabin, grabbed Goree's body by the shirt collar and dragged it inside. Then he went back outside to Maribel, and they stood together for a long while watching the flames slowly take over the cabin and grow finally to engulf it. They watched the blaze devour what had been their little home. They listened to the roaring, the rushing sounds, the crackling and the occasional loud pops. They stayed until the cabin caved in from the fire, then they mounted up, and leading Neosho's horse as a pack animal, began the trip to Riddle, Iowa, on the far side of the dividing line. Blue didn't know what would become of Maribel, but for now he would see that she was safe. Later, if he survived, he'd think more about it.

Snake Perrine, followed by his five companions, walked into the front of Blanch's saloon. While the other five headed straight for the bar, Snake looked around the room until he spotted Cutter Macklin, then made his way straight across the room to Macklin.

"Cutter," he said, "where's Avant?"

"Up in his room, I think," said Macklin, and he turned and headed for the stairs, followed by Snake.

From behind the bar, Blanch watched them climb the stairway to the rooms above. She hadn't seen Avant since Abel Kane had left her under the bed on the floor of Avant's room. She wondered whether or not her partner had discovered that he had been robbed. She wondered if she should tell him what she knew. She wondered if she would. Kane was a dangerous man. She wasn't sure she could trust Overton Avant to protect her from Kane, and then, too, she had opened the safe for Kane. What if Avant found that out? He had a terrible temper. Why, she asked herself, had she opened the safe for Abel Kane? She had been afraid. She had thought that he was planning to kill her. That was why. And she hadn't had time to think clearly. But it had been a mistake. She should not have opened it. Why, he wouldn't have shot her right in the hotel in the middle of the day. Someone would have heard the shot. And that, Blanch knew, was what Avant would say. She shouldn't have opened the safe.

Upstairs in his pink room, Overton Avant sat submerged in a deep tub of steamy water. The bubble-bath suds rose to his chubby chin, and occasionally he sliced through them with the sides of his fat hands, picking bubbles up on the back of a hand, then puffing them away into the air with a short breath. He heard a knock at his door.

"Who is it?" he shouted.

"It's Cutter and Snake," came the voice from out in the hall. "Snake and them's back from that chore you sent them out on. He's got important news for you."

"Snake and them?" said Avant to himself. "What about Goree?"

He was irritated at this interruption of his bath, but it sounded as if the news might be urgent. He would have to see them. He would see them in a few minutes, he decided. He would not let them in while he was in his tub.

"Go back down and send Blanch up here," he shouted toward the door. "I'll send for you in a while."

In a few minutes, Blanch let herself into the room with her key. As soon as she shut and relocked the door, Avant stood up in his tub. Bubbles clung to him all over. He held his arms out to his sides. Blanch picked up a large towel, and stepping around behind him, wrapped him in it and began rubbing him to dry him off. His pudgy flesh shook with the rubbing. Avant lifted first one pink foot and then the other for Blanch to dry, as he stepped out of the tub and onto the plush carpet.

"Help me get dressed, Blanch," he said, "then go downstairs and send those two clods back up here to talk to me."

Overton Avant greeted Snake and Cutter in his usual fashion—sitting fully dressed in his overstuffed chair, smoking a cigar and sipping champagne.

"So," he said when the two came into his presence, "was the mission successful this time?"

"Neosho's dead," said Snake, his face expressionless.

"Good," said Avant. "Good. Where's Goree? Why isn't he reporting this to me?"

"He's dead too."

"Dead? How did it happen?"

"Neosho got him before we got Neosho."

Having given thus much of the truth, Snake thought but a moment before he went calmly on.

"Neosho shot his jaw off," he said, "and Chicken blowed him away with his shotgun. Said he didn't want to watch him suffer."

"What about Neosho's partner?" said Avant.

"We never seen no sign of him."

But Blanch had followed the two men back up to the room, and she had just entered the room in time to hear Avant's last question and Snake's answer to it. She thought about her accidental encounter with Abel Kane and about the possibility of Avant's discovering who had opened the safe for Kane. She was afraid that he would never understand why she had done it. She knew that he wouldn't, but she felt like she had to do something.

"I know who he is," she blurted out so suddenly that she wondered why she had opened her mouth.

Avant stared at her in disbelief.

"Just how in the hell would you know anything like that?" he said.

"I know," said Blanch.

"Well, all right then. Who is it?"

"It's that man who calls himself Abel Kane," she said.

Now Blanch knew there would be no backing out. She had to make this good. Avant was advancing on her, his pudgy face turning red.

"What?" he said. "How do you know?"

Avant's tone of voice and his facial expression betrayed building anger. He had, after all, just offered the man a job. This was a direct affront. His judgment of character, a thing he prided himself on, was being challenged. Blanch knew Avant well. She knew how this news was affecting him. She thought quickly. She didn't want to get herself into deeper water by spouting off too quickly and without thinking. Above all, she didn't want Avant to know that she had opened the safe for Kane, even at gunpoint.

"I saw them together once," she said. "I just remembered it. Just now put it all together. And that Kane, he's a stranger here. He had to come from somewhere. He's got to be staying somewhere. Neosho's got a partner. It all adds up. It has to be him."

"Hmm," murmured Avant, stroking his second chin. "I wonder."

"He was up here, too," Blanch added as an afterthought.

Avant whirled back toward her.

"Up here? When? In this room?"

"He was up here after he left you. I don't know if he was in this room or not. I don't suppose he was. The door is always locked. But I saw him leave by the back stairs, so I know he was up here."

Avant rushed to the door like a mad bull and jerked it open. His face was red and puffy.

"Get out of here," he shouted. "You two get out."

Blanch was proud of her cleverness. She had worked things out just fine. As the two gunslingers left the room, Avant turned on Blanch.

"Open the safe," he ordered. "Quick."

Blanch opened the safe again with trembling hands. She wondered if her ruse were working. She had to convince Avant that Abel Kane was the man he was after without letting him find out how she actually knew. She got the safe opened, and Avant shoved her aside. He dropped down on his well-padded knees in the pink carpet to look into the safe.

"No. No," he shouted. "He was here. I've been robbed. He's robbed my safe. He was in my own room. How could this have happened? Get those two back here. I want them to kill him. I want him dead. He was here."

It was early morning when Coleman Miller unlocked the door to Miller's Emporium in Riddle, Iowa. The sun was not yet up, and had Miller not known the layout inside so well, he would have needed a light to find his way back to the office. He relocked the front door behind him, for he would not be ready to open up for business for some time yet, and made his way to the office in the back of the store. He unlocked the office door and stepped inside. A gaslight was mounted to the wall just inside the door. Miller struck a match, turned on the jet and lit the lamp. As he turned around to go to his desk, he saw a rugged-looking cowhand sitting across the room. Beside him was a girl—a young woman really. If she'd had a bath and a change of clothes, she might have been pretty, he thought. An impulse caused Miller to reach for the right-hand desk drawer where he kept a pistol, but before he could get the drawer opened, the stranger's voice stopped him.

"I wouldn't do that, Mr. Miller," it said.

Miller froze in position, one hand on the desk drawer, leaning forward. He looked up at the stranger. The stranger's gun was pointed at him.

"I don't want to hurt you, Mr. Miller. I need your help."

"This is a peculiar way of going about asking for help," said Miller.

"Yes, I know, but I have no choice. Now I'd like for you to just step around to this chair over here and sit down please."

Miller walked around to the chair that stood at the left of his desk for visitors to his office to use. He turned it to face the stranger, then slowly sat down.

"What do you want with me?" he asked.

"Mr. Miller, do you know what happened to Brice Seagraves over in West Riddle?"

Miller was startled to hear this rough-appearing range bum mention the name of the manager of the traveling Shakespeareans. It was a few seconds before he answered.

"Yes," he said, "I believe so. He was robbed by that bunch of crooks who run the town. They took everything he had, I understand, before they let him leave town. What has this got to do with you—or me?"

The stranger stood and walked over to Miller's desk. He still held his six-gun in his right hand, but in his left he was carrying a cashbox. He set it before Miller on the desk.

"Open it," he said.

Miller reached for the cashbox and opened it up. He looked inside, then back at the stranger.

"I think that's all Brice lost," said the stranger. "I got that out of Overton Avant's private safe. You know how to contact Brice?"

"Why, yes," said Miller, "I have his New York address right here in this desk. Besides, we're right on his way back at the end of the tour. He told me that he would stop back through for a visit. Why?"

"I want you to give this money to Brice. I may not be able to do it."

"All right," said Miller, "but . . . "

The stranger interrupted him.

"Now are you convinced that I didn't come here to do you any harm? Can I put up this six-gun?"

"Yes. Yes, go ahead. If you had come to rob me, you wouldn't have brought your own cash, I suppose. Who are you? What's your interest in Seagraves?"

The stranger shoved his pistol back into its holster and sat back down.

"I've been most recently known as Abel Kane over on the other side of the line, but you knew me in Riddle as Tyrone Hamlin."

"What?" said Miller, coming halfway up out of his chair, then slowly settling back down. "Yes. Yes. By God, I can see it now that you've told me. I'd never have guessed it otherwise, though. By God, it's amazing. Hamlin, huh? Hamlin."

Miller broke into laughter. When the laughter died down, the actor continued.

"I've another favor to ask of you."

"Oh," said Miller, wiping his eyes. "Oh yes. What is it, Hamlin? Hamlin."

He chuckled and shook his head.

"This lady here is Maribel," said Blue Steele. "She had a man. We called him Neosho."

"The cowboy? I know who he is. You said, 'had.' "

"Avant's men killed him. She needs a safe place to stay until I can take care of some business across the river, and then—well, we'll see then. Can you put her up in a nice room? Get her some decent clothes? See that she gets her meals?"

He reached into his pocket and pulled out some loose bills which he handed to Miller. Miller put the money on the desk.

"That should cover the expense," said Blue. "If it doesn't, I'll settle up with you when I get back—if I get back. I don't know just how long all this will take."

Miller thumbed through the bills. He looked at Blue Steele.

"Of course," he said. "Don't worry about her. She'll be well taken care of. But what are you going to do? You're not thinking of taking on Avant's crowd, are you?"

"I'm going to kill every one of those sons of bitches."

"That's a dangerous job, Mr. Hamlin."

"Someone needs to do it, and I've got nothing to lose."

Miller stood up and walked around behind his desk. He reached for the center drawer, but before grabbing hold of it, glanced up at the actor.

"All right?" he asked.

"Sure. Go ahead."

Miller opened the drawer and pulled out the old copy of the *New York Times.* He tossed it on his desk. It was folded to reveal the photograph of John B. Temple.

"I know," he said. "Good luck to you, Mr. . . ."

"Abel Kane will do for now."

". . . Mr. Abel Kane."

Miller extended his hand, and Blue Steele took it in his and squeezed it. Miller picked up the money off the top of his desk and extended that toward Blue.

"You don't need to pay for her keep," he said. "Let's call that my contribution to your project."

"Thanks," said Blue. He pocketed the money, then he turned to Maribel.

"Don't you worry," he said. "Mr. Miller will take good care of you until I get back. And if I can, I will be back."

Then he turned to Miller again.

"Be seeing you," he said.

As he turned and walked out the door, the sun was just beginning to peek over the horizon.

Blue Steele was riding back toward West Riddle. As he nudged his mount onto the Missouri River bridge, he saw Snake Perrine and Mike McKinney loom into view at the opposite end of the bridge. Blue hefted his six-gun to make sure it was sliding in its holster. He was too far away yet to recognize the two men over in Nebraska. He urged his horse forward slowly. At the other end, Snake spoke to McKinney.

"Is that Kane?"

"I can't tell yet," said McKinney. "It could be."

"Come on," said Snake, and he began riding toward the dividing line in the center of the bridge. McKinney rode slowly a little behind and off to Snake's right.

"Don't get too close to the middle," said McKinney. "Make him come over to this side. Avant said we shouldn't never cross the middle of that bridge."

"Shut up," said Snake. "Is that him?"

Mike squinted.

"That's him. That's Abel Kane, for sure."

Over on the other side at about the same time, Blue Steele recognized McKinney and Perrine. He didn't know their names, but he knew them to be part of the gang that he was after. He halted his mount. Perrine and McKinney did the same. For a moment, the only sounds to be heard were the tramping and pawing of horses' hooves on the bridge, the puffing and blowing and snorting of the horses and the soft murmur of the Missouri River below. Then Snake Perrine broke the silence.

"You Abel Kane?" he said.

"Who's asking?"

"We work for Mr. Avant in West Riddle. Mr. Avant would like to see you."

"I've got no business with Avant," said Blue.

"He thinks different. He says you robbed his safe. We're deputies. We're going to take you in."

"I ain't on your side of the line. Not yet."

"You come on over, slow and easy, or I'll bring you over," said Snake.

"Don't do it, Snake," said McKinney. "You can't cross over."

"Shut up, Mike. You coming, Kane?"

Blue Steele thought about the gunfighter in St. Joseph. He smiled. He felt good.

"Come and get me," he said, and he began to slowly back his horse away from the center of the bridge. "Come on, you long string of slime."

Snake Perrine jerked out his pistol at the same time as he spurred his mount, and he raced toward Blue Steele.

"God damn you," he shouted, and he fired a shot at Blue. It went wild.

"Don't do it," shouted McKinney. "Come back, Snake."

Snake fired again, and Blue Steele felt the bullet whistle close by his ear. He dismounted, and letting his reins trail, drew his six-shooter calmly, stretched out his arm in front of him and took aim at the figure racing at him in a fit of rage. Snake fired again, and the bullet tore up splinters a few inches from Blue's right boot. Blue squeezed the trigger. His bullet tore into the upper right chest of Snake, shattering the right scapula as it ripped its way out the back. Snake screamed in pain and rage. His horse screamed in terror and reared up, lunging sideways at the same time, and horse and rider went crashing through the rail and plunged over the side of the bridge beginning a long and graceful flight to the river below.

McKinney was turning his horse to race back for the security of West Riddle, but Blue Steele had climbed aboard his mount as soon as he had fired and was coming fast at McKinney. By the time McKinney had turned around and lashed at his animal, Blue was beside him, crowding him, pushing him against the railing. McKinney was terrorized. He had the picture of Snake Perrine sailing through the air in his mind, and he didn't want to follow Snake into the cold, dark river. He lashed at his horse. He lashed at Blue, but his pursuer reached for a knobby stick that hung from a loop on his saddle and belted McKinney across the chest with it. McKinney fell backward out of the saddle, his horse still racing toward West Riddle. McKinney's left foot caught in the stirrup, and McKinney dangled between the frightened animal and the bridge rail. He was being dragged unmercifully, the bridge and the rail raking him, tearing his flesh, filling the raw, fresh wounds with ragged wood splinters. McKinney screamed. Blue slowed his horse and let the other get well ahead of him. He could see over in West Riddle several figures moving about. He couldn't tell who they might be, but it was no longer safe, if indeed it ever had been, for him to ride on across. He turned and rode back to the Iowa side and headed out toward the farm country. He hadn't had any trouble with the law in Iowa so far, and he didn't want to have any. It was best to avoid Riddle.

So Avant was on to him, he thought. It must have been

Blanch. Of course, she had told Avant that she had seen him. She had probably told Avant who had robbed his safe. Otherwise McKinney and Perrine wouldn't have been waiting to challenge him on the bridge. He would have to find another way into West Riddle. He would need a new approach to Overton Avant. As he rode along, he pulled the penknife out of his pocket, removed the pistol from its holster and carved a fourth notch onto the handle. He tried to count in his mind the men who would still be working for Avant. How many would he have to deal with? He remembered that he had been passed on the road by six men. The man he had just killed and the one with the hide full of splinters were two of them, he believed. Six and one down. That leaves five of that batch. Five. Then there were the two he had met in Blanch's saloon. What were their names? Cutter something and—shitface. Cutter and shitface were all the names he could remember. Well, that's two more, he said to himself. Five and two. Seven. Seven and Avant. But they'd be after him now for sure, and they'd be watching every trail. They would, especially, be watching the bridge.

He had to get back on the other side of the river, and he had to attack. But how? And where? He no longer had any place to hole up, and he was utterly alone. He thought of Neosho and wished that the cowboy were there with him to plan the next move and help carry it out. He thought of the possible outcome. If he were to be successful in wiping out the Avant crew, who would enjoy the results? A bunch of mice in West Riddle, but not Neosho. The original reason, the purpose of this attack, was gone. There was no longer anyone to return the ranch to. Seagraves' money was already restored, or soon would be. Even Maribel had said that it didn't matter anymore. Then Blue recalled seeing Neosho lying in his own blood, shot in his sickbed by some degenerate wretch with a shotgun, and he remembered his promise to the dead man. He remembered why he had intended to continue this fight until the end, and he recalled a passage from scripture: "Vengeance is mine, saith the Lord."

"No, Lord," he said. "Not this time. It's going to be mine."

Mike McKinney was lying naked on a bed in a spare room in Blanch's saloon. He was on his face, and he was whimpering and crying like a baby, as West Riddle's combination barber, dentist and horse doctor was busy picking splinters from his raw, mangled flesh. An open whiskey bottle stood on a bedside table, and now and then the Doc would pick it up, take a drink, and pour a little over the ground meat of McKinney's backside. Each time he did, McKinney would howl with pain. Overton Avant came into the room.

"Tell me what happened," he demanded.

McKinney sniffled.

"Tell me what happened," repeated Avant.

"I'm hurt," said McKinney. "Let me be."

Avant pushed the Doc aside. He picked up the whiskey and slopped it all over McKinney, making the suffering man writhe in agony and scream with pain. When McKinney tried to turn over, wounds on the other side were exposed and the whiskey got them, and the turning aggravated the awful sores and caused the as yet unextracted splinters to stab and gouge him the more. Avant quit pouring and McKinney eased himself back into his original position.

"Now," said Avant, "do you think you can tell me what happened out there on the bridge?"

"It was Kane," sobbed McKinney. "Me and Snake seen him. He was coming over. I told Snake to wait, but he wouldn't. He crossed over. I told him to come back. He didn't listen to me. Kane killed him. Blowed him and his horse right off into the river. I run, but he caught me. He made my horse drag me on the bridge."

"What about Kane? Where's Kane?"

"I don't know," whined McKinney. "I didn't see nothing after the dragging started. How could I?"

Gurnsey stepped in out of the hallway.

"I seen it from over here," he said. "Kane rode back across to the other side."

"Damn," said Avant.

Gurnsey was holding a riding quirt in his hand, and Avant reached for it.

"Give me that damn thing," he said.

He took the quirt from Gurnsey and gave the raw, bleeding butt of McKinney a vicious lash. McKinney screamed. Avant handed the quirt back to its owner.

"Fools," he said. "I want to see everyone downstairs. Now."

In a few minutes all of Avant's gunslingers except McKinney were gathered around him in the saloon. Blanch was behind the bar, but near enough to hear what was said. Avant was pacing. He was puffing furiously on a cigar. Sweat was running down his face, and his clothes were soaked. Avant was afraid. First there had been Alfalfa George, then Goree and now Snake Perrine. And his own room had been broken into and his personal safe robbed. He wasn't secure. He felt surrounded by fools and incompetents, but there was no one else for him to turn to. If it were to become known that he couldn't control West Riddle, West Riddle would be taken away from him. It would be taken over by somebody else. He had to depend on these men. There was no other choice. He looked them over. Who was left? The only one who came near having any brains anymore was Cutter Macklin. Macklin would have to be promoted. He faced his small army.

"Men," he said, "Cutter is in charge. Now listen to me carefully. I'm in danger. We're under attack by this Abel

Kane. Cutter, I want this place guarded at all times. I want
two men in the hallway upstairs watching my room. I
don't want Kane or anyone else getting in there again.
Two men, you hear? And I want three down in this room.
The other two can be out in the street. I wish we could
spare some to send out looking for this—Abel Kane, but I
can't afford to let this place go unprotected."

"He's over on the other side, Mr. Avant," said Gurnsey.

"I know, you fool," shouted Avant. "You said that. But
that doesn't mean that he won't come back. And for all we
know, there might be more of them. All we knew about at
first was Neosho. Now it's Abel Kane. What next?"

He took a deep breath to compose himself. Then he
went on.

"The men out in the street will watch the bridge. I want
to know about anyone who crosses that bridge. Cutter,
take care of it."

Avant headed for the seeming security of his pink room,
leaving Cutter Macklin with his new command. Cutter
sent Gentry and Gurnsey to follow Avant up the stairs and
guard the hallway. He told Chicken to go out and watch
the bridge. Then he saw that there were only three of
them left, and he had been told to keep three men in the
saloon. But he was supposed to have two out in the street,
and had only sent Chicken. He decided that he, himself,
would take the other end of the street, and the third man
inside would have to be McKinney. McKinney would just
have to suffer his wounds and stay at his post. This was a
serious situation. It was an emergency.

McKinney was dressed with a great deal of agony. It
seemed that his whole body was a raw, bleeding sore. The
weight of his pistol belt around his waist caused him much
pain, but when he was finally dressed, he decided that he
had only thought he knew what pain was until he tried to
walk with clothes on. Negotiating the stairway was particularly excruciating. But eventually McKinney was at his

post at one end of the bar. He got himself a bottle of whiskey to ease the pain a little. Damn, he thought. He wanted Abel Kane to come through that door. He wanted to see him shot to death. Or better, just shot down, not dead. He would scratch him to death. He would cut the head off the body and kick it down the main street of West Riddle. He would. He would do all that if he could get his hands on Abel Kane. He would do it—just as soon as his sores all healed up. Yes.

CHAPTER EIGHT

Blue Steele made a lonesome camp alongside the Missouri River on the Iowa side, several miles north of Riddle. He built a small fire, and he made some coffee. He had learned to be a pretty fair gunslinger. He could ride a horse well enough. He could pass as a Westerner all right, but one thing he wasn't yet prepared for was carrying the right provisions along for cooking on the trail. He was hungry, but the coffee would have to do, he guessed. This was a fine life he had laid out for himself—the man who had been on the verge of overshadowing the great Booth. He leaned back on one elbow and sipped some coffee from his tin cup. He thought of his triumph as Richard Humpback. Good God, it had been fine. He wanted to play Hamlet. That was, of course, the dream of every actor. But he had brought his own acting career to a halt, and Hamlet must go out of his mind. He would never play Hamlet now. No, his latest role was Abel Kane. He hoped that it would not be his last. If he lived through it, the next would be—who knows?

He had to pee, and even though he was all alone at his little camp, he didn't feel like standing up in the light of the fire to do it, so he walked a little ways off into the shadow. A rabbit jumped up and ran a few steps away. Blue Steele whipped out his six-shooter and fired a rapid shot which sent the cottontail somersaulting forward. Blue trotted after the creature and retrieved it. He tossed it back toward the camp fire and finished what he had gone to the shadows for in the first place. Then he went back to the fire. He picked up the rabbit by its ears. It was pathetic-looking, limp and bloody. Blue had never cleaned a rabbit, but his mind reached back to his childhood, and he remembered watching Chickenhawk do the job neatly and deftly. It had seemed easy. If he had only paid closer attention, he thought, if he had only been allowed more time with Chickenhawk . . . He had not been allowed to become a hunter or even a fisherman.

But he was hungry. He pulled out his penknife and set to work. He made a mess of the job and almost made himself sick in the process. He thought that he wouldn't want to eat the rabbit after what he had put it through, but he made a spit anyway and set the flesh to roasting over the small fire. Small fire. Hum, he thought, he had retained some lessons from Chickenhawk. White men make fires too big, Chickenhawk had always said. Indians make small fires. A small fire is all you need. Soon the smell of the roasting rabbit meat caused Blue to forget both the past and the mess he had made a few minutes earlier. He even forgot the temporary nausea he had suffered over his butchering. He was, after all, hungry, and the cooking meat smelled good.

He ate the rabbit, put out the fire and rolled up on the ground to sleep. Soon he would have to find a way across the river and back to West Riddle. He would have to plan his attack. He had a vision of himself as some sort of avenging angel, riding fast down the main street of West Riddle, a gun in each hand and the reins of his mount in his teeth, blasting every ugly sonofabitch that moved on the street. He drifted off to sleep with this image in his head.

They were on the sidewalks and on the rooftops, and each time he fired one fell. He kept shooting, and they fell. Then he was standing calmly on the board sidewalk and shooting slowly and deliberately. Bullets nicked the boards at his feet, shattered the window glass behind him. He heard them whistling past his ears, but he remained calm, and each time he fired, one fell. Suddenly one was riding hard down the center of the Missouri River bridge, and the gunfighter fired both pistols at once. Horse and rider toppled over the edge of the railing and sailed through the air in a wide arc. He was standing on the bridge and watching as they got smaller and smaller hurtling toward the dark waters below. When they disappeared, there was no sound—only silence. He turned and found himself again on the street. There were bodies all around him, but he was no longer the black-suited gunfighter, nor was he Abel Kane. Standing there in the midst of the carnage he, himself, had created, he was the child, Blue Steele.

Overton Avant did not sleep well. He kept running out into the hallway to demand of his guards whether or not they had seen or heard anything suspicious. When they informed him that everything was quiet, he roared at them that they were not being vigilant enough. He was too nervous even to enjoy his usual perverse diversions. There were seven men guarding him from this madman, Abel Kane. What had he ever done to Kane? Nothing. Why, he had even offered Kane a job, hadn't he? Who was this Kane anyway? Where had he come from? What was his interest in all this? And where in the hell was he? What was he waiting for? If he wanted a showdown, why the hell didn't he come riding on into town and have it out? Avant was ready, by God. He was ready for Abel Kane. He glanced up and down the hallway to get a reassuring look at his guards. He strode over to the top of the stairway and looked down into the saloon to see the guards there. He could see Simp and Poppen sitting across from each other at a round table playing cards. McKinney sagged in his chair at the far end of the bar, a bottle of whiskey in the grasp of his left hand. Avant's face turned red.

"Wake up down there," he screamed. "God damn you. Watch that door."

He hurried back to his room, slammed the door behind him and locked it. Yes, by God, he was ready for Abel Kane. But why didn't Abel Kane show himself? Why didn't he come?

A week passed, and still Abel Kane did not show. For the first three days, Avant had alternately cowered and fumed. Then he had developed a cautious calm. The fifth day he became cocky. By the end of the week, he not only had decided that Abel Kane was not going to show up at all, he was boasting to everyone that he had frightened the man out of the country for good. He relaxed his guard. He, himself, relaxed. He began to indulge in his favorite perversions again.

Blue Steele dressed as Abel Kane rode into Riddle and tied his horse in front of Miller's Emporium. Inside, Maribel was dusting the shelves, having just sold a bolt of cloth to one of the upstanding ladies of the community. There were no other customers at the moment. She was thinking what a difference there was between the two towns, and yet how close together they were. Riddle was such a respectable little community with fine businessmen like Mr. Miller. Mr. Miller had been good to her. He had gotten her a room in a boarding house and had given her a temporary job in his establishment. He hadn't really needed the extra help. She knew that. She knew that he had only given her the job to help her out. The bell over the front door jingled, and Maribel looked up to see Blue walk into the store. Blue was pleased at her appearance. She was well dressed and looked generally good. He tipped his hat.

"Howdy," he said.

"Abel."

Maribel ran to Blue and hugged him. The suddenness of it startled him.

"I'm so glad to see you," she said.

"Is anything wrong here?" asked Blue.

"No," she said. "Mr. Miller has been real nice to me. It's just that I don't really know him—or anybody else around here. I'm just glad to see you, that's all. Okay?"

Blue shifted his weight and shoved the Stetson back on his head.

"I ain't done over there yet, Maribel," he said. "With that business, you know? I still have to go over there and finish what I promised I'd do. I just came by to see how you're doing."

"Don't go back," said Maribel. "You don't have to."

"I do have to," said Blue. "I can't explain it to you if you don't already understand it, but I have to do it."

"Abel," she said, her voice sounding a protest.

"Let's not talk about that," he said. "That's not why I came in here today. What time do you get off work? I thought maybe we could have dinner."

"Yeah," she said. "I get off at six. But let's not go to a café. We put out some real nice picnic baskets right here at Miller's. Let's get one and go off somewhere. I don't want to be around a bunch of people. Okay?"

"That sounds just fine, Maribel," said Blue.

They built a small fire along the east bank of the Missouri, and they boiled coffee. They ate the ham and boiled eggs and the rest of the stuff in the Miller picnic special, and they relaxed. They talked small talk. Maribel did not ask him what he planned to do in West Riddle nor when he planned to do it, and he did not volunteer his thoughts on that subject. They both knew, however, that he had no intention of walking away from the situation. Avant and crew were responsible for everything rotten that had happened there. Blue finished his coffee. He got up and smoothed the blanket he had been sitting on, then he stretched out on it. Maribel moved to his side. She lay down close to him. She put an arm across his chest and snuggled her head into his shoulder.

"Do you mind?" she said.

"Maribel," said the actor, "there's no way I'd mind having you close to me, but in my head, you're Neosho's woman."

"Neosho's dead, Abel. We have to go on. We're alive."

He turned toward her and put a hand on her cheek. He kissed her tenderly on the lips.

"I'm not Abel Kane, you know," he said.

"Oh, that's right. I just seem to want to call you that. You're J. B. Temple. Is that right?"

She kissed him, a little longer than the first kiss, and her lips parted slightly. He put his arms around her and held her close, and an image of another white woman long ago intruded on his mind.

"So what do I call you?" she said. "J.B.?"

"If you like."

He rolled away from her and laced his fingers behind his head, staring up at the bright stars in the clear sky. He saw the Milky Way and recalled a story from his childhood about a dog and some spilled cornmeal.

"Where the dog ran," he said.

"What?"

Suddenly he stood up and paced away from the fire. He stood on the slight rise staring at the waters of the Missouri River as they raced along on their endless journey. Maribel watched the clouds drift past his head.

"What's wrong?" she said.

He turned to face her, and he thought about his long-ago hopes for Grace and how they had been dashed because of who—of what he was. He recalled the beating and the suffering he had endured for having dared to long for a white woman, and he thought of the years of assumed identities—identities assumed to hide the truth.

"Maribel," he said, "I'm not Abel Kane."

"I know," she said.

"And I'm not Tyrone Hamlin. I used to be J. B. Temple, an actor in New York who's wanted for murder."

Maribel was puzzled at Blue's suddenly peculiar behavior. He still stared at the river. She decided to stay quiet and let him talk.

"It doesn't matter," he said. "I'm not even him. I made him up along with all the others."

There was a long silence. He stared into the rushing waters. She watched him silently and wondered who he might be. She felt as if the face that belonged to the man she thought she knew was no longer there. She wondered what he would look like if he turned back to face her again.

"Who are you?" she said.

He took a deep breath and turned, and Maribel was relieved to see the face she knew.

"I'm a Cherokee Indian," he said. "My name is Bluford Steele."

He told her the whole, long story of Bluford Steele, of Grace and of Reverend Wiget, of the beating at Hanover and of his revenge. And as he unfolded the tale he noticed that he was beginning to feel a strange sense of relief from a burden long carried. When he had finished with his story, Maribel held out a hand toward him.

"Come here," she said.

He walked back to the blanket there beside her and sat down. She reached for him and pulled him close to her.

"It doesn't matter," she said. "I love you, Bluford Steele."

"Maribel," he said. "I hope you do. I think you need some more time."

Overton Avant had just come from his bubble bath. He had on fresh silk underwear and a fresh white suit. He was powdered so heavily that the powder still rose from his pudgy flesh when he walked. He was puffing a cigar, and in his right hand he carried a glass of champagne. He strolled to his favorite chair in the saloon and sat down. Cutter Macklin walked over to his table.

"Sit down, Cutter," said Avant. "Sit down."

Cutter pulled out a chair and sat.

"I ain't heard nothing about that Abel Kane," said Macklin.

"Of course, you ain't," said Avant. "That pantywaist is probably in St. Louiee by now. Folks around these parts know better than to mess with Overton Avant. He knew that I was after his rotten hide, and by God, he skedaddled."

Avant emptied his glass with a gulp, then he held it high over his head to signal the bartender to come running. Just as the barkeep was filling Avant's glass, Poppen came in the front door.

"Mr. Avant?" said Poppen.

Avant sipped his champagne, set the glass down, then folded his fat, pink fingers across his great paunch. He looked up at Poppen.

"Yes?" he said.

"Mr. Avant, they's an old German outside. He says he's a farmer, and he's looking for a spread. He's got some cash. I couldn't get him to say how much, though. He can't hardly talk good English. Just off the boat and come straight out here, I guess. I ain't sure I understood him good."

"Bring the man in, Mr. Poppen," said Avant. "The real estate office is open."

"Yes sir," said Poppen, and he turned and hurried back out into the street. Avant jiggled his glass at the bartender again and got himself a refill.

"You got a farm to sell?" asked Cutter Macklin.

"Hell, yes, Cutter," said Avant. "How about the old Neosho place?"

"That ain't no farm," said Macklin. "Neosho run cows up there, and there ain't no house on it. It's burned down."

"I heard it was a farm," said Avant. "And I ain't seen no ashes. The last I heard there was a nice little house out there."

Poppen came back in followed by a bent man in overalls and brogan shoes.

"Come on," said Poppen. "Over here."

Poppen strode to the table where Avant and Macklin waited. The other followed more slowly. His head was ducked. He held his cloth cap in both hands in front of him. His corduroy jacket was covered with dust, and his long hair and beard were both greasy and tangled. He almost shuffled over to Avant, approaching the table as if he were in court, approaching royalty.

"This here's the German, Mr. Avant," said Poppen.

"How do you do?" said Avant, a big smile widening across his face. "Sit down, sir. I'm Overton Avant. And what might your name be?"

The German, if indeed he was German, kept his eyes on the floor. He answered Avant in a low voice.

"I am Friedrich Arthur," he said, "chust come from Homburg, sir."

"Sit down, sit down, Mr. Arthur," said Avant.

The farmer, for he certainly had the appearance of a farmer, reluctantly dragged out a chair and perched on its edge. He kept it well away from the table.

"Relax, Mr. Arthur," said Avant. "You're among friends here. We like to welcome new members to our little community. Have a drink. What do you like to drink?"

"I tried some rye viskey in Saint Looie," said Arthur. "It vas goot."

"Get Mr. Arthur some rye whiskey, Cutter," said Avant.

"Go on. Bring the bottle. And while you're at it, bring my bottle over here, too."

Cutter got up and walked over to the bar. He brought back two bottles and set them on the table.

"Cutter," said Avant, "where on earth were you raised?"

Macklin gave him a perplexed look for an answer.

"Get some glasses, Cutter. Get some glasses. We have a guest here."

Macklin headed back for the bar once more, and Avant smiled a ludicrously phony sweet smile at the prospective property buyer sitting on the edge of his chair.

"I have to tell him every move to make," he said.

Cutter Macklin brought the glasses. He placed one in front of Avant and poured some champagne. Then he poured the other two full of rye whiskey, handed one to Arthur and sat down with the other one for himself. The German sipped at his glass gingerly.

"Thank you, Cutter," said Avant. "I understand you're a farmer, Mr. Arthur."

"In the old country I vas a farmer," Arthur answered. "I grow rice, unt I make beer. It's goot beer. Now I need some goot land to grow my rice unt start here mit der beer."

"I have a couple of nice little places you might be interested in, Mr. Arthur. Not too far out of town. Good rich land, near the river."

"Near the river is goot," said Arthur.

"I could have Cutter, here, take you out tomorrow and show them to you. It's a little late in the day right now, and I expect you've had a long trip. Why don't you get yourself a nice room for the night, and you can ride out and look at these places in the morning?"

"Dat sounds goot to me. Tank you, sir."

"I think you'll find the prices right, especially when

you've seen the land. I don't think that you'll find a better deal anywhere in the country."

"I don't know American prices," said Arthur. "Maybe it vill be too much for my pocketbook."

"Don't worry about a thing," said Avant. "We can work something out. You're in America. The land of the free and free enterprise. Our credit system is a wonder, an absolute wonder. Anything is possible in America. This is the greatest country in the world, Mr. Arthur. If you stay here, you'll soon find that out. Now you just leave everything to me. You get a good night's rest and meet Cutter here in the morning. Just go right through there to that desk, and you can get yourself a real nice room for the night."

Arthur took one more shot of rye whiskey, bade the others good night and left to get a room. As soon as he was out of sight, Avant began to chuckle.

"I'll bleed that goddamned Dutchman for everything he's got," he said.

"I thought he was a German," said Cutter.

"German, Dutchman, who gives a damn? What's the difference between a Dutchman and a German anyway?"

Cutter Macklin scratched his head.

"I don't rightly know," he said, and he reached for the bottle the German had left behind. "Anyhow, what do you want me to do with him in the morning? You want me to leave his bones out there and bring back his money?"

"No, you stupid fool," said Avant. "As far as you're concerned, this here is a legitimate real estate transaction. You show him Neosho's place and the old Washburn place. Then bring him back here to me. And be nice to him. You hear me? He may be worth more if I string him along for a while. Come to think of it, I might just let him stay. I wouldn't mind at all having a nice little brewery around here."

About three o'clock that morning, Mike McKinney was walking stiffly along the river front by the bridge. His body still ached, but the excruciating pain was gone. Avant had relaxed, but he hadn't abandoned his guard altogether. He still insisted on keeping a guard on the street at all times. McKinney resented having been assigned guard duty so soon after his ordeal. He was still sick. He was in pain. He had been hurt bad by that Abel Kane. Avant had said that Abel Kane was gone. Lit out. By God, McKinney hoped not. He wanted to kill that Kane—slowly. He wanted to mutilate his body. He wanted to make him scream the way —well, the way McKinney had screamed. McKinney stepped stiffly up onto the bridge and looked across to the Iowa side. He shivered just a bit remembering the fateful encounter with Abel Kane that had occurred out there in the middle. He looked over his shoulder to see if anyone was in sight. He saw no one, so he reached into his coat pocket and drew out a bottle of whiskey. If Cutter caught him drinking while he was on watch, he would be all over him. Maybe even report him to Avant. *Damn Avant,* he thought. *Damn him all to hell.* He was in pain and he needed a drink. No one was around anyway, and even Avant kept saying how they had run Abel Kane out of the country. He tipped the bottle up and emptied it. There hadn't been much left in it.

"Hell," he said.

He walked over to the bridge railing and pitched the empty bottle into the dark waters below. Watching the bottle disappear into the darkness, he thought of Snake Perrine and Snake's horse arcing into infinity, and he shuddered. Though the sight gave him the willies, it also fascinated him. He leaned his hands on the railing. Suddenly a strong hand grabbed his shirt collar and held him forward.

"Hey," he shouted.

He struggled, but the hand was powerful, and in spite of

himself, McKinney couldn't take his eyes away from the darkness below. He felt something long and hard thrust itself between his legs, and in the darkness, he caught a glimpse of a knurly cane which reached from his crotch to the top of the bridge rail. The hand pressed against the back of his neck, and the rod was wedged between his legs with its head resting on the rail. It pressed up into the crevice between his buttocks, and it crushed one testicle. He struggled against the two separate pressures on two different parts of his body. The pain between his legs caused him to forget the old pains in his body, and the terrible dread of the black waters of the Missouri River down below almost overshadowed all other pain altogether. He snarled and tried to twist around to face his attacker. He thought of reaching for his gun, but he was afraid to take his hands off the rail. Then suddenly the pressure on his neck ceased, but before he had a chance to react to this new freedom, the lower end of the rod was raised with tremendous force. Its head was still on top of the rail, and McKinney's attacker was using the cane as a fulcrum. McKinney was flung over the rail, and he went sailing into the darkness with a long diminishing scream.

The old German was just making his way toward the table where he had met with Overton Avant and Cutter Macklin the night before when something in the tone of the voices he heard made him pause. The same two men he had sat with the night before were there again, and their voices were agitated. He strained to hear what they were saying.

"Well, where is the sonofabitch?" snapped Avant.

"I don't know, Boss," said Cutter. "I had him on guard duty last night, and whenever Poppen went out to relieve him this morning, he wasn't nowhere to be found."

"The bastard run off," said Avant. "Send someone after

him. No one runs out on me. Bring him back here dragging from the end of a rope. Bring him back here alive."

"Boss," said Cutter, "I don't think he run off."

"Oh, you don't? Why the hell not? Answer me that."

Avant remembered how he had tortured poor McKinney in his rage the day the wretch had been dragged on the bridge. He knew that McKinney had good reason to want to leave his employ. Still, it didn't look good having his hired hands desert him, especially since they knew too much about his activities. He couldn't allow quitting.

"His horse is still in the stable," said Cutter, "and there ain't no other horse missing neither, not since George's horse disappeared a while back. And his rifle's propped up against the bridge rail down there."

"Oh?" said Avant, a look of worry slowly replacing the one of anger on his fat face. He had a sudden unsettling thought about Abel Kane.

"Besides that," Cutter Macklin continued, "payday's tomorrow. If he was going to run out on us, he'd of waited till after he got his pay. He wouldn't a gone last night. Not him. He was broke, too. I know that."

Avant had turned away from Macklin during this last speech and was rubbing the edge of the table nervously with his fat, pink palm. There was a moment of silence before he slowly turned back to face his latest top hand. He raised his beady eyes toward Macklin. Fear was in his expression. The pink had drained from his cheeks, and his whole fat face was pale white.

"You don't think . . . ?"

"Abel Kane," said Macklin.

"No," screamed Avant, smashing his fist on the table. "No. No. No."

Friedrich Arthur from Homburg stepped up to the table, his hat in his hands.

"I'm sorry to be eavesdripping," he said. "I don't mean

to, but I couldn't help it. I heard. There is some killer loose?"

Avant saw in his mind the German's greenbacks floating away from his grasp, and he struggled to compose himself.

"Mr. Arthur," he said, sweat running down his round cheeks and dripping down onto his white shirt front. "Good morning. I'm sorry you had to hear that. There's really no reason for you to be concerned. There is a criminal loose. Yes. We thought that he had left the country, but it appears that he's come back. Mr. Macklin here is the sheriff, though, and he's going to be hot on this man's trail. Don't you be worried. The good citizens of West Riddle will be protected. Now why don't you go on out with Mr. Macklin and take a look at that land?"

"But Mr. Macklin needs to be looking for dat badman. I can't be making problems for de sheriff mit a killer loose."

"It's all right," said Avant. "He's got some deputies out right now at this minute searching for the fugitive. He's got the time for you right now. Just run along with him now, and don't you worry none. You hear? Run along now."

"Mr. Avant's right," said Cutter Macklin. "Come on and I'll show you them places."

Macklin led the way out, and Arthur followed him. Outside there was a buggy waiting. Macklin motioned Arthur to climb up into the seat, then he went around to the other side and climbed in, taking up the reins. Avant stood in the doorway of Blanch's saloon and watched them drive out of town toward the Neosho property. A brewery would be a nice thing to have, he thought. Then the image of Abel Kane reappeared in his mind. He looked around himself impatiently and yelled out.

"Poppen. Gurnsey. Where the hell is everybody?"

By ten o'clock in the morning, at Miller's Emporium in Riddle, Iowa, Maribel had been at work for two and a half hours. It had been a busy morning. She had measured out any number of yards of cloth for the local ladies, had sold a goodly amount of staples for the kitchens of the community and even some small hardware. There was a lull in the bustling morning's business. It seemed to stop all at once. No customers were in the store. Maribel decided to restock the shelves where the items had sold particularly well. She was busy putting up canned peaches when Coleman Miller came out of his office. Miller's other employee, a young man named Hiram, was sweeping. Miller went to the shelves where Maribel was working. She was a hard worker, he thought, and she had suffered so much in her young life. He was glad that Hamlin or Kane or whatever he called himself had brought her to him for help. It did his heart good to think that he was in some small way improving the life of this fine young lady. In fact, Miller was beginning to develop fatherly feelings for the girl, an interesting development in that Miller, at fifty-six, was a confirmed bachelor. He watched her for a moment.

"Maribel," he said, "let's take a break. I need a cup of coffee. Why don't you join me?"

Maribel kept putting peaches onto the shelf.

"I'm okay, Mr. Miller," she said. "Really, I'm not tired at all."

"You're working too hard, Maribel. You need to take a break every now and then. Come on."

"Mr. Miller, I know that you really just gave me this job as a favor. You didn't need no extra help. I intend to work for my keep."

"I know you do, and you have been, but you still need to take a break every now and again. Besides that, if you refuse to admit that I'm right, I'll put it to you another way. I need a break. I need to get out of the store for a few minutes, and I hate to drink coffee by myself. Won't you please join me across the street for a short break? Keep me company?"

Maribel finally stopped working as if she had to get all the cans of peaches onto the shelf by a deadline which was fast approaching. She looked at Miller.

"Well," she said, "since you put it that way, I guess that I should join you. Just a short break?"

"Yes," said Miller. "A short one. Let's go. Hiram can watch the store while we're out, and when we get back, he can take himself a break. Okay?"

"Okay."

They crossed the street to a small café and went inside to a table by the window. Miller could keep an eye on his establishment that way. He didn't tell Maribel his reason for selecting the table, however. He ordered coffee and apple pie for each of them. He felt a remarkable sense of accomplishment at having pulled the girl away from her work. For some reason, and Miller couldn't quite put a name to it, he felt a tremendous need to do things for Maribel. He had given her a job and settled her in a nice room. He saw to it that she had new clothes. (For that he had been forced to tell Maribel that he was giving her an advance on her pay. She had refused to allow him to spend any money on her.) Still he felt like he should be doing more. And he wondered why.

It must have something to do with West Riddle, he decided. He had long felt guilty about the existence of that place across the river. Of course there was nothing he could do about it. But something inside him told him that by ignoring the sin and the crime so close to his home, within walking distance from his place of business, by allowing it to continue, he was somehow condoning it. He was not a man of action. He was a businessman. Now Maribel had some kind of connection to this strange Abel Kane who had turned out to be the actor, Hamlin, and Hamlin, or Kane, for some reason or other, was about to take on the entire criminal element of West Riddle. By doing all he could for Maribel, Miller reasoned, he was helping to accomplish that all-important task. *Yes,* he thought, *that must be it. I am doing something about that den of iniquity after all.* Having worked his way through all that convoluted psychology to analyze his sense of responsibility toward Maribel, Miller concluded that, even so, she was still a lovely young lady, and he was just as glad that she was his opportunity to help. The waitress put pie and coffee in front of Maribel and Miller and trudged on about her business.

"It looks good," said Maribel.

Miller took a bite, chewed and swallowed it.

"It is good," he said. "Maribel, will you stay in Riddle?"

The question took her by surprise. She looked at Miller for a moment.

"I don't know," she said. "I haven't thought much about it, I guess."

"You don't have any plans?"

"No. Not really."

"You know," said Miller, "you can stay if you want to. You can work for me as long as you like. It's true that I created the job for you as a favor, but now that you've been working, I can see that I should have hired someone extra long ago. Business is good. You can see for yourself how busy things have been around the store."

"Yes," said Maribel. "It has been busy. I like it that way."

"Oh, I do too. I'll never complain about good business. But you see that I can use you? You can stay if you want to."

"I really don't know, Mr. Miller. I don't know what I want to do. I appreciate what you said."

"Do you have . . . ?"

Miller paused in the midst of his question. He sipped at his coffee.

"Yes?" said Maribel.

"I started to ask something that's probably none of my business."

"Go ahead," said Maribel. "It's all right."

"This man, Kane or Hamlin or whoever he is . . ."

"I call him Abel. He said to call him Abel Kane, so I do. He said his real name is . . ."

Maribel hesitated. Blue had originally told her and Neosho that his real name was John B. Temple, but more recently he had confided in her that he was in fact a Cherokee Indian named Bluford Steele. She didn't know whether or not she should let that last information slip to Miller. Perhaps she would be betraying his confidence.

"His real name is what?" said Miller.

"John B. Temple," said Maribel.

"Yes, I know about his real identity," said Miller. "I've known for some time. There was a story in the New York *Times* which I received in the mail. His photograph was in there, too."

"Then you know about the killing he done in New York?" said Maribel.

"Killing?"

Maribel was suddenly afraid that she'd said more than she should have said. The story must not have been about the killing, and she had let it slip. She was angry at herself and embarrassed. She flushed slightly. But there was no going back now. She had said it, and it was done.

"Yes," she said. "He killed a man in New York. That's why he changed his name and came out west. It was in a fight, and the man was trying to beat him to death. He stabbed the man. He was just defending himself."

"Oh, my God," said Miller.

"What? What is it?"

"It all makes sense now."

"What?"

"The reason he left New York and keeps changing his names and identities. It makes sense. Maribel, he obviously thinks that he killed that man."

"You mean he didn't?"

"No. I read the story. He cut the man all right. He did that. But the man didn't die. In fact, he wasn't even too badly hurt. According to the story, there are not even any charges. The man admitted to attacking him in his dressing room. Apparently our actor thinks that he's a fugitive from justice."

"Oh, that's wonderful news," said Maribel.

"Except for one thing," said Miller.

"What's that?"

"Maribel," said Miller, "do you remember what he said to me in my office when he first brought you over here? He said that somebody had to take on that bunch in West Riddle and that he didn't have anything to lose. Do you remember that?"

"Yes."

"Well, then, don't you see? He thinks that he's a wanted murderer anyway. That's why he thinks he doesn't have anything to lose. If he knew the truth, do you think he'd be doing all this?"

Maribel bit her lip and pondered Miller's question for a long moment.

"We've got to tell him," she said.

"Maribel, we don't know where to find him. I never did ask you that question. The one I said was probably none of my business anyway."

"Oh," said Maribel. "Well, what is it?"

"Is there something special . . . ? That is, what do you feel for this man?"

Maribel looked down at the table. She was silent for a long moment. Miller decided that he shouldn't have asked, and he was about to tell her that she needn't answer —that he was sorry he had said anything. Then she spoke.

"Mr. Miller," she said, "I was in love with Neosho. I was living with him. I guess that's wrong, but we were going to get married. We had plans. And I loved him."

She paused and took a sip of coffee. Miller wondered

again if he shouldn't have minded his own business, but he was concerned about the welfare of this girl. He had to know what was what if he were going to help her out.

"Well, now Neosho's gone," said Maribel. "They killed him. And Blue . . . I mean Abel Kane has been so good to me, and he was around when I needed someone and I didn't know anyone else. Well, Neosho hasn't been gone all that long, I know, but I think that I love Blue, uh, Abel. I love him. Do you think I'm crazy? Or bad?"

"No, Maribel. No," said Miller. "I think you're a fine young lady. I don't think you're crazy or bad, and I don't think there's anything wrong with your feeling love for this man. But you said 'Blue.' You said it twice. What did you mean by that?"

Maribel had done it again. She had let something else slip. But Miller knew that Blue was not a murderer, so maybe it was all right she told herself. And he was helping them. Well, she might as well tell him everything this time.

"His real name is Bluford Steele," she said.

"What? Are we still talking about the same man?"

"Yes."

"John B. Temple, Tyrone Hamlin, Abel Kane? That man?"

"Yes."

"Bluford Steele, did you say?"

"Yes. That's his real name. He just told me. He told me the whole story, and until right now, I think that I was the only person in the world who knew. He's a Cherokee Indian, who . . ."

"Whoa. Hold on a minute," said Miller. "He's an Indian?"

"Yes sir. His mother was a white woman, and she raised him most of his life because his daddy was killed. And she sent him off to college somewhere up north, I don't know its name, and when he left there, he went to New York and changed his name to be an actor. That's when he started to call himself John Berringer Temple."

"And when Temple thought he had killed a man, he had to leave New York City. Then he became Tyrone Hamlin. Right? I think I'm beginning to see the light. Maribel, your young man is a remarkable individual. Do you know that?"

"Yes," said Maribel, "I think I do, but I'm afraid he's going to get himself killed over there, Mr. Miller. I'm afraid."

Macklin had driven the German immigrant, Friedrich Arthur, out to the Washburn place. Arthur had looked it over and poked around, muttered something about the soil being too dry and generally grumbled around. Then Macklin took him to what had been up until recently the home of Neosho and Maribel—and Abel Kane. When they crossed the property line onto the place, Macklin stopped the buggy.

"This here's where the property starts," he said. "It goes clean down to the river on this side and then way over yonder. I'll show you the other boundary after a while."

"Dat's fine," said Arthur.

Macklin drove on. They kept going until they came to the spot where what was left of Charlie Hall lay unburied, unmourned and unattended except by small scavengers. Macklin cursed under his breath. He had forgotten about Charlie, but it was too late. The damned German had already seen him. He should have gone the long way around. *Damn,* he thought.

"Vat is dat?" said the German.

"That? Why, uh, I don't know," stammered Macklin.

"Stop der buggy. Dat's a dead man."

Macklin hauled in on the reins, and Arthur jumped down from the front seat. He trotted over to the remains.

"It's a dead man, all right," he said. "Vat kind of place is dis?"

Macklin thought for an instant about pulling out his six-gun and killing the German, but Avant had said to be nice to him. Avant had plans for him. He wanted a brewery somewhere around. Well, he could be killed later if necessary.

"Well," he said, "it must be that killer we're looking for. He must a done this. This kind of thing don't happen around here all the time. We got us a killer loose right now is all, but we're going to find him, and then you won't see no more of this kind of thing. Don't you worry none. Climb back up here, and let's go on ahead and get you a look at this place."

Macklin was proud of his speech. He thought that he'd played the sheriff's role remarkably well. He wished that Avant could have seen him.

"You are de sheriff, nein?" said Arthur. "Ve can't chust leave dis here."

"We can't help him none now," said Macklin. "I'll have some of my boys come by here in a little while. Come on, now."

Macklin was desperate. His imagination was running dry. He was supposed to be nice to the German, and he was supposed to show him the property. Yet he was also supposed to be playing the role of a lawman, a role which he didn't really know how to play. One good speech had been about all he could handle. He wanted to hurry up and get the job done and get back to town to find out from Avant what to do. Damn all this thinking anyway. He'd rather just shoot at someone any day.

"Come on," he said.

Arthur climbed back up onto the seat mumbling, and Cutter Macklin, who had suddenly broken out into a heavy sweat, whipped up the horses. He was headed straight north with the intention of showing the German the northern boundary of the property.

"Drive over dat vay," said Arthur, indicating the tree-lined hills off to his right which masked the riverbank.

Macklin groaned and headed for the trees. They drove on in silence for a few minutes.

"Stop here," said Arthur.

Macklin stopped, and the farmer jumped down out of the buggy.

"What do you want out here for?" said Macklin. "There ain't nothing here to look at."

"Of course dere is," said Arthur. "Dere is hills und trees. De river is right t'rough here, no? Dis flat out here is so dry. If I buy dis place, I vant to know vat is vat, you know? I vant to valk in here some. Check soil. Moisture. See vat grows here. I von't be long. You need to get your poys up here pretty soon. I know dat. I von't keep you long, sheriff."

Arthur walked into the woods on the very footpath which led up to the old Neosho cabin. *Damn,* thought Macklin. *How'd he come to pick just this damn spot?* Macklin jumped down to follow him. *Maybe he won't go too far in there. Maybe I can distract him in another direction. How the hell did he happen to pick just this damn spot anyway?* Macklin instinctively tested the heft of his six-gun, checked its looseness in his holster. *God,* he thought, *I may have to kill this old bastard if he sees something he shouldn't! Avant will sure be mad as hell if I do, too.* He followed along behind the old German as the latter trudged, sniffed the air, bent occasionally to examine some wild plant which was to Macklin just another goddamn weed, and then ambled on further. *Goddamn German,* thought Macklin. *And he's so damned worried about the law. Hell.* Then the farmer stopped abruptly in his tracks, and Macklin nearly ran into him. *I've let him go too far,* he thought in a panic.

"Py golly, look," said Arthur. "A house vas burnt here."

"Oh, yeah. That's right," said Macklin. "I did hear something about that, come to think of it."

He felt stupid. Avant was right, he thought. He was stupid. He couldn't figure out why he said what he said, but he couldn't figure out what else might have been better.

"Vat you heard?" said Arthur.

"Oh, nothing much. Just that the old house up here had burned down, that's all."

Macklin pulled out a bandanna from his hip pocket and mopped his brow.

He's asking too damn many questions, he thought. *I'm going to have to kill him if he don't shut up!*

"But vait," shouted the German. "Look. More killing vas here."

Macklin was in a furious sweat. What would Avant want him to do? He dragged the bandanna out of his back pocket again and mopped his face with it.

"Oh, yeah? Well, I guess it was that goddamned Abel Kane again. That's that killer we're looking for. That's his name. Abel Kane. My boys will look into it. I mean, I'll come back out here and investigate right after I get you safe back to town."

"Vy not inwestigate now? Ve are here?"

"I got to think of your safety first. You're a citizen. Well, are you? Anyway you will be pretty soon when you buy some property. I'll come back later. It ain't right to get innocent citizens mixed up in no investigation."

"Und vat vill you look for ven you come back?"

"Why, I'll look for evidence, a course. Everybody knows that. Don't they look for evidence after a crime where you come from? Hell, I'll look for evidence. Yeah. I'll see if I can find out who that is that's been killed, and then I'll find out if I can who done it."

"I think you already know all that."

Macklin whirled to face the new voice. The German dialect had vanished. The old farmer was standing there facing him, his hands tucked into the bib of his overalls. He was staring hard at Macklin.

"You—who are you?"

"You know me as Abel Kane."

Macklin went for his gun, but before he could clear the holster, Blue Steele's right hand came out from under the bib of the overalls with a fistful of blasting six-gun. The first slug tore into Macklin's groin, the second sliced him a new navel, and the third crushed his sternum and flung him sprawling on his back in the ashes of what had been Blue Steele's temporary home. As Macklin's body thudded into the refuse, a black cloud of ash dust rose up around him. Blue Steele reached into a pocket and took out three bullets. He dropped the empty shell casings from his pistol to the ground and reloaded, stuck the pistol back under the bib of the overalls and turned to walk back down the path to the waiting buggy.

Overton Avant was flopped in his easy chair panting heavily. His face was a mask of mingled rage and fear. He had two guards in the hall outside his room, and his patience was running thin. He wanted to see the body of Abel Kane. A mere report of the man's death would not be enough. He needed to see the body—to make sure. He had never seen Neosho's body. What if those incompetents had lied to him? What if Neosho was still alive and out there somewhere with Kane? *You can't trust anyone,* he thought. *Not anyone. Damn them all. When I get this Abel Kane business taken care of, I'll show them, by God. I'll get rid of all of them. Replace everyone. Damn it to hell. I've got to see Kane dead!* He thought he would hang the body up somewhere to rot—someplace where he could look at it every once in a while to reassure himself that all was well—that he was still in control. He had to stay in control. Without control of his financial empire he would lose all his power and be nothing—worse than nothing. Physically, Avant was helpless. He had been soft all his life, and he had led a self-indulgent life which had kept him flabby. As a child and a young man he had been bullied and ridiculed. The power of his empire protected him from that. He couldn't bear the thought of ever having to endure the insults and the bullying again.

There was a knock at the door. Avant jumped up as fast as his bulk would allow and hurried to his desk. He pulled out a drawer and removed the little two-shot derringer. Dropping the pistol into a coat pocket, he turned to face the door.

"Who is it?" he demanded.

"It's me."

He recognized the voice of Blanch.

"Well," he shouted, "come on in then."

He didn't move to open the door, so Blanch had to let herself in with her key. Avant abruptly brushed his way past her and into the doorway where he looked nervously up and down the hall. He had turned to go back inside the room when he heard a shot from out in the street. The two men in the hallway jumped up from their chairs.

"What the hell was that?" said Poppen.

"I don't know," said Gurnsey. "A gunshot."

Three more shots followed, then shouting. Avant shoved Gurnsey out of his way and ran down the hall to the top of the stairway. He called down to Chicken who was posted at the front door of the saloon.

"What the hell is going on down there?"

Before Chicken could answer, Blue Steele in his disguise as Friedrich Arthur, the German farmer, came bursting through the front door of the saloon, a gun in his hand. He looked frantic.

"Help. Help," he shouted. "De killer is coming. Abel Kane is coming. Somebody do something, qvick."

Blanch poked her head out into the hallway from her position inside Avant's private room.

"Get down there, you two," she shouted to the gunmen in the hall. "There's trouble."

Gurnsey and Poppen hesitated.

"Downstairs," she screamed at them.

Gurnsey and Poppen ran past Avant and down the stairs into the saloon, as Avant shouted over the balcony.

"Watch the street," he yelled. "Get that Dutchman up here."

Blue hurried up the stairs obediently, and Avant grabbed him by the arm and hustled him down the hall and into the pink room. He shut the door and locked it behind them, then turned panting to face Blue.

"What the hell are you talking about?" he demanded. "How do you know Abel Kane?"

"I don't know Abel Kane," said Arthur, "but he is coming. I know dat. You must do something before he comes here."

"Now you just calm down," said Avant. "Get ahold of yourself. How do you know he's coming here?"

"Mr. Macklin, your sheriff, he said it vas Abel Kane. Ve vas attacked at de farm vere he vas showing me. It vas a nice farm. I like de river bottomland. I tink I could grow my rice dere, all right, und . . ."

"Oh, shut up about the farm," said Avant. "We'll talk about that later. What about Abel Kane?"

"Oh, ya. Vell, Mr. Macklin is a real hero. You should be very proud of Mr. Macklin. Poor Mr. Macklin."

"What about Abel Kane, damn it?"

"Mr. Macklin told me to get back to town. He stayed to fight dis killer, Abel Kane. He said it vas Abel Kane. Dat's how I know. Ve vas attacked, und Mr. Macklin told me to come back."

"But you said Abel Kane was coming here?"

"Dat's right. As I vas running for de buggy, I heard him

shouting to poor Mr. Macklin, 'I'll kill you, den I'm going to town for de others.' Dat's vat he said."

"Maybe Macklin got him," said Avant. "You said you left and they were fighting."

"No. No. I said dat Mr. Macklin told me to get out and come to town vile he stayed to fight dat killer. I couldn't leave poor Mr. Macklin to fight by himself. I ran toward de buggy, but I stopped in de trees and bushes and vatched to see if I could help. Mr. Macklin is dead. I saw him shot by dat Abel Kane. Maybe Abel Kane did not know I vas dere, because he didn't hurry avay from vere he killed de sheriff, but I did. I hurried back to de buggy and drove fast to get here and varn you to get ready. He is coming. 'I'm going to shoot dat fat pig, Avant.' Dat's vat he said. I heard him say dat."

The color that remained in Avant's face drained at those last words. He shoved a pudgy hand into his coat pocket and gripped the derringer. His hand was sweating.

"All right. All right," he said. "You get on out of here. You can go. Find yourself a safe place to hide."

"I go," said Blue.

"Wait a minute," said Avant. "Unless you want to use that there gun you're carrying around to help guard the streets."

Blue moved toward the door.

"I help, py golly," he said. "I saw dat killer shoot poor Mr. Macklin. I help."

Blue left the room and headed down the hallway, and Avant once again locked himself in. He paced the floor nervously. *He wants to kill me,* he thought. *Me. I never done a damn thing to Abel Kane. I don't even know Abel Kane. What the hell does he want to bother me for? Why? Who the hell is Abel Kane anyway? My boys will get him. By God, if he tries to come into my town, my boys will get him for me. I'll hang him up right out front. Right on the main street for everyone to look at. No one will ever dare to cross me again. No one! Damn Abel Kane!*

Across the river in Riddle, Iowa, Coleman Miller and Maribel were walking back to the store from their coffee break when they heard the three shots. They stopped in their tracks and looked at each other.

"Oh, God," said Maribel.

An old farmer coming toward them on the sidewalk stopped and looked in the direction of the river bridge.

"There they go again," he said. "They're at it agin in West Riddle. Too bad they don't just kill each other off and have it done."

The door to the marshal's office opened and Sergeant Bluff Luton stepped out onto the sidewalk. He stared toward the bridge, then ambled out into the middle of the street. Miller moved to join him, followed by Maribel.

"Morning, Coleman," said Luton. "I still can't seem to get used to it."

"What's that?" said Miller.

"Hearing that gunfire so close and just setting here and ignoring it. It just don't seem right that there's nothing I can do."

"It's the law, Bluff," said Miller.

"What do you mean, there's nothing you can do?" said Maribel. "You're the marshal."

"Maribel," said Miller, putting a hand on her shoulder, "he's the town marshal here in Riddle. He's got no jurisdiction—no authority—outside of town. Even our county sheriff couldn't do anything. West Riddle is outside of the state."

"That's crazy," she said.

"Sometimes I agree with you, little lady," said Luton.

"But Blue might get killed."

"Blue?" said Luton.

Miller looked as if he had been caught at something, and Luton caught the look. He turned to face Miller directly.

"Maybe you better tell me what's going on," he said.

Miller sighed and looked at Maribel. Her expression told him nothing about the question in his mind, so he decided to go ahead and confide in Luton.

"You remember Hamlin?" he asked.

"Yeah."

"Well, Blue is Hamlin."

"You want to run that one past me again?" said Luton.

"The man we knew as Hamlin is really named Bluford Steele."

"I thought he was this Temple from New York."

"I did too, Bluff," said Miller. "It seems that Bluford Steele has been going around under several different identities over the last few years. I just found out from Maribel. But the thing we're concerned about right now is that Blue Steele is over there in West Riddle all alone determined to clean out that nest of rattlers."

"What?"

"That's right," said Miller.

"And he could get himself killed," said Maribel.

"Damned quick and easy," said Luton.

"Well, then," said Maribel, "can't we do something?"

"Damn it," said the marshal. "No. We can't. We can't do a damn thing. Come on."

Luton led the way in long strides to the river bridge. Miller kept up with him fairly easily, but Maribel had to run to keep from being left behind. When they reached the bridge, Luton walked up onto it and continued until he reached the middle.

"Stop here," he said. "This is the dividing line. We can't go no further."

"Well, what are we doing here then?" said Maribel.

"We're going to watch," said Luton. "Just watch."

"I don't have to stay here," said Maribel, but before she could run across the line, Miller grabbed her and held her.

"Maribel," he said, "I won't let you go over there. You might get hurt."

"Let me go," she said, struggling against his grip.

"No. Listen to me. What do you think it would do to Blue if you went over there? He'd be worrying about your safety. You'd get him killed for sure."

Maribel's struggle to get free grew half-hearted and finally ceased.

"All right," she said. "You can let go of me. I won't go."

Over in Blanch's saloon, in the upstairs hallway, Gentry was standing near the railing overlooking the saloon downstairs. Simp had gone to the far end of the hall and stepped out onto the small landing on the backside of the building overlooking the alley. The actor in his Friedrich Arthur disguise stepped out onto the landing with Simp. With a worried look on his face, he looked first at one end of the alley, then the other.

"You tink dat killer come dis vay?" he said.

"He might," said Simp. "You never know."

"Py golly," said Blue, "I tole Mr. Avant I help. I have dis pistol. Py golly if dat Abel Kane comes down dis alley, I blast him good. I vill."

"You'd have to shoot faster than me to get him first," said Simp.

"Look dere," said the actor, pointing a finger suddenly toward their left and down the alley.

"Where?" said Sim, drawing his six-gun and stretching his neck in the direction Blue had pointed. "Where? What do you see?"

Standing behind Simp, Blue raised his six-gun high over his own head and smashed it into the back of Simp's, knocking him cold, at least, and sending him over the railing and crashing into the alley below. Simp lay still.

Then Blue climbed up onto the rail and reached for the overhanging roof. He tugged and kicked and finally pulled himself up onto the roof of the building. Crouching low, he ran to the front overlooking the street. Anticipating trouble, everyone had cleared the street—everyone except Avant's guards. Blue eased up to the edge of the roof and peered over. Chicken was visible directly below. He was standing just outside the front door to Blanch's saloon, holding his shotgun ready for action. Blue reached inside the bib of his farmer's overalls and pulled out a cowboy's lariat. Remembering the man called Gill in New Hampshire, he snaked out a loop and dropped it through the air, hauling back on it just in time for it to snag under Chicken's chin. He pulled hard, and the loop tightened around Chicken's neck. Chicken gagged and spit. He felt total panic. He pulled the trigger of his shotgun and blasted a hole in the wooden sidewalk beneath his feet. Blue drew Chicken, kicking and hacking, up a few feet off the sidewalk, lapped the rope around the chimney, and ran for the edge of the building. The next building over was only a few feet away and had a lower roof than did Blanch's saloon. He jumped for it, ran across the low roof and dropped into the alley.

The shotgun blast brought Gurnsey running out the front door of the saloon, and he ran right into the dangling feet of Chicken.

"God damn," he shouted, and he jumped back inside.

"What is it?" said Poppen.

"Chicken is hanging out there," said Gurnsey. "Somebody strung him up."

"Somebody, hell," said Poppen. "Abel Kane."

Both men drew their guns and held them ready. They looked nervously toward the street, backing slowly toward the bar at the back of the big room.

Out on the bridge, just across the dividing line, a group of citizens from Riddle had gathered around Maribel, Miller and Luton. All were craning their necks, trying to see something of what was happening in their neighbor town.

"You say he's cleaning up the town?" said one.

"One man?"

"Never happen," said the old farmer who had warned Brice Seagraves on his first drive through Riddle. "They'll kill him. Maybe have already."

"No," said Maribel, "they can't kill him." Then more to herself than to anybody else she added, "They just can't."

Miller put an arm around Maribel's shoulders. He felt utterly helpless. Bluff Luton stood stiff, clenching and unclenching his fists down at his sides. He was itching to get in on the action, but his sense of the law held him back.

Upstairs in the saloon, Blanch unlocked the door to the pink room and burst in on Avant who was holding out at arm's length the little pocket pistol, his hand trembling, his face colorless, his white clothes soaked with perspiration.

"Don't shoot, damn it," said Blanch.

"What's happening out there?" said Avant.

Blanch could hear the fear and desperation in his quavering voice. *The disgusting little bastard,* she thought. *He's nothing without his hired guns. And his money. His money.*

"Everyone's dead except Gurnsey, Gentry and Poppen," she said. "They're all in the building."

"Three left? Just three?"

"Just three. That's all."

"Where is Abel Kane?"

"Nobody's seen him, but he's out there somewhere."

"Send those three cowards out there to get him," said Avant. "What am I paying them for?"

"Overton," said Blanch, "if they go outside to look for Kane, who's going to guard you in here?"

Avant no longer held the little pistol out in front of him. His arms dangled loosely at his fat sides. His whole body sagged.

"What am I going to do, Blanch?" he whimpered.

"We've got to get out of here," she answered. "We've got to get the money and get across the bridge where there's some real law."

Blanch rushed to the safe and hurriedly worked the combination. She took out handfuls of money and stuffed it into Avant's pockets.

"But Kane's out there," said Avant.

"And he'll be in here before long. If we stay, he'll get us for sure. Maybe those three will keep him busy long enough for us to get out of here. Come on."

Blanch led the way out into the hall. There they paused and looked carefully in both directions before moving out onto the landing overlooking the alley. They looked up and down the alley, then hurried down the steps and ran through the alley until they arrived at the livery stable. Blanch hurried inside with Avant puffing along behind her. Lewis was in, but Blanch and Avant did not see him. He had climbed up into his loft and was hiding behind a stack of hay bails.

"Get a buggy," said Avant.

"I don't see one. Let's saddle up a couple of horses."

"Damn you," said Avant. "You know I can't ride a horse. Hitch up that wagon there."

While Blanch led the horses to the wagon and worked to get them hitched up, Avant was peeking out a front window trying to get a glimpse of his nemesis. He could see nothing in the street. His sweaty right hand was in his coat pocket clutching the derringer.

"Damn it, Blanch," he said, his voice low and intense, "hurry it up, will you? Hurry."

Downstairs in the saloon, Gurnsey too had run out of patience.

"I'm going out there after that sonofabitch," he said.

Poppen stood still, his eyes on the front door.

"Be careful," he said.

Gurnsey eased himself out the front door, being careful to avoid the dangling feet of Chicken. He held his gun in his hand, cocked and ready to fire. He looked up and down the street, then began to move cautiously along the street in a direction away from the river. A movement at the end of the block caught his eye, and he jerked the gun up to fire. A man had just stepped out from behind the corner building. When Gurnsey recognized the German farmer, he expelled a long sigh, released the hammer and lowered his pistol.

"Hey, farmer," he shouted.

"Ya?"

"You see anybody down that way?"

"Vat you say?"

"Is anybody down there, damn it?"

"There's none but I, devil's butcher."

"What?"

Gurnsey's slow brain couldn't decide what to make of the farmer's changed voice, but he wasn't the type to take time to think. He was puzzled, and to his way of thinking, the best way to deal with a puzzle was to eliminate it— quick. He jerked up his gun again and thumbed back the hammer. As he pulled the trigger and sent a bullet smashing into the wall beside his target, Blue Steele pulled his six-shooter from inside the bib, pointed and fired. The slug caught Gurnsey in the throat, ripping out the back of his neck. He stood for a moment, wobbling on his feet, the pistol dangling from his limp fingers, his head bobbing loosely on his shoulders as if it would fall off, a stupid, bewildered expression on his face, then, all at once, he pitched forward onto the sidewalk. Blue reloaded his six-gun.

Not counting Blanch and Avant, for they would be no problem with the others out of the way, there were only two left, he thought. He believed that they were inside the saloon, but he didn't know just where they would be. They could be in the hallway upstairs or in the main room downstairs. They could be in a room somewhere. They might be together or they might be in different spots. They were probably hiding, cowards that they were, hoping to shoot him from ambush. His advantage, of course, was that, so far as he knew, no one had yet connected the German farmer with Abel Kane. No one except Macklin and Gurnsey just before they died. He decided to retrace his steps back to the landing in the alley. If no one was in the hallway, he could break in Avant's door and use him to get the others.

On the bridge Bluff Luton had begun pacing. The talk of the crowd was getting loud and it made him even more nervous than before. Suddenly he turned to face the fidgeting group of Riddle citizenry there behind him.

"Hold it down a minute, folks," he said. "Be quiet for a minute. I have something to say."

The murmurs slowly died down, and Bluff continued.

"How many of you folks are carrying a gun?" he said.

Two men held up their hands.

"Let me see them," said the marshal.

The two men, both young and somewhat rakish-looking, reached under their jackets and pulled six-guns out of their belts. They held them up for Bluff Luton to see. Bluff let out an exasperated sigh and scratched his head.

"All right," he said, "you two move up here in front, and hold them things up so they'll show. We need a few rifles."

Miller stepped forward.

"I've got rifles in the store," he said. Then he turned to

survey the crowd on the bridge. Hiram had abandoned his post at the store to join in the excitement, and Miller spotted him.

"Hiram," he said, "run back to the store and grab a handful of those new Winchesters and bring them right back here. Hurry."

"How many?" said Hiram.

"Three or four is enough," said Luton.

"Bullets?" said Hiram.

"No," Luton snapped.

"Get going, Hiram," said Miller, then he turned to Luton.

"What are you up to, Bluff?" he said. "Rifles and no bullets?"

Bluff Luton held up his hands for silence again.

"Nobody fires a shot," he said. "Anybody who fires a shot will be arrested. Is that clear? I mean it. Anyone shoots, I'll put his ass in jail."

"Well, what the hell do we want with guns then?" asked one of the two young men with pistols.

"Listen to me," said Luton. "There's only one man over there fighting that whole damn bunch of thieves. We keep hearing shots. That means, the way I take it, that they ain't got him yet. If he's getting them, it seems to me like someone might try to get over here for safety. If that happens, just stand here and make those guns obvious as hell and look mean. But don't shoot."

The actor reached Avant's room and took hold of the doorknob. Cautiously, he turned it. He heard nothing from inside the room, and he was surprised to find the door unlocked. He pushed it open and stepped aside. Still nothing. Leveling his six-shooter for action, he jumped inside the room. No one was there, and the safe was standing open. They had apparently cleared out.

"Damn," he muttered.

He went back out to the hallway and started toward the inside stairs at the opposite end. He paused at each room, opened the door and looked inside. Each time he found an empty room. No Avant. No Blanch. No one. He had one room left at the end of the hall. If anyone was upstairs, he would find them in that room. He eased the door open and it creaked loudly on its hinges. Gentry's voice sounded from below.

"Who the hell is up there?"

The actor quickly showed his face over the rail.

"Chust me," he said.

"It's that goddamned German," said Poppen.

"He makes me nervous," said Gentry.

"Kill the sonofabitch," said Poppen.

"Hell, all right."

Gentry jerked his pistol and fired a shot at Blue Steele, who dropped quickly behind the railing. As he fell to the floor, the actor pulled out his gun. He fired between the uprights of the railing, the bullet passing through Gentry's ear and on into his head. Gentry fell like a sack of flour. Poppen had taken a dive behind the bar and was out of sight. There was a long moment of silence. Then Poppen's voice came rising up from the floor below.

"Hey, mister. What are we fighting for? Hell, I don't even know you."

"You know me," came the answer. "You know me as Abel Kane."

"You?" said Poppen.

The sound of a wagon moving fast on the street carried into the saloon, and Poppen looked out the window. He saw Avant and Blanch racing a wagon toward the river bridge. He jumped up, forgetting about Abel Kane, and ran for the front door.

"Hey," he shouted. "Hey. You can't leave me here, Avant."

Poppen ran out into the street with the actor vaulting

down the steps after him. When the actor hit the front door, Poppen had just grabbed the reins to a handy horse standing at the hitching rail. He saw the actor come through the door, and he turned to face him. The actor fired once, hitting Poppen in the chest, grabbed the horse and mounted, turning him to race after Avant and Blanch. They were about to reach the bridge, and the actor knew that he couldn't overtake them in time. Once they reached the dividing line, he would be in trouble. He couldn't kill Avant over there without arousing the wrath of Sergeant Bluff Luton and Iowa law, and he couldn't catch them and turn them over to Luton or any other Iowa law officer because they hadn't broken any laws over there. He couldn't afford to let them reach the line. His sensitivities balked at the thought of what he had to do, but he could think of no alternative. He jumped out of the saddle and took a careful aim. Pulling the trigger, he knocked down the horse on the left. The animal screamed and dropped, causing the other to stumble, and the wagon overturned throwing Blanch and Avant into the dirt. Blanch landed with a thud and lay still for a moment. Avant rolled over and over in the dust. The actor ran for them. Avant was trying to scramble to his feet and at the same time gather up bills that had fallen from his over-stuffed pockets. He looked up to see the actor rushing for him. He gave a last longing look at the money still fluttering in the dust and ran for the bridge. Blue Steele raised his pistol to shoot just as Avant stepped onto the bridge. Steele hesitated and Avant ran ahead. Steele aimed again, but before he pulled the trigger, he saw Avant come to a sudden stop. On the bridge, Avant had seen the crowd of heavily armed Riddle citizens waiting for him at the other end. There was the town marshal, Sergeant Bluff Luton standing right there with them. He looked over his shoulder at Blue Steele, then back at the crowd ahead of him.

"You got to let me come across," he shouted at the crowd.

There was no answer from the crowd, no reaction to his demand.

"You're the law," he shouted.

The crowd just stood there holding up rifles and hand-guns and looking menacing. Avant turned to face Blue Steele. He saw that the actor had walked up closer to the bridge. Frantic, he pulled the derringer from his pocket and fired one shot. It was wide. The actor knew that the little gun had one more shot. He raised his pistol and fired. A small red spot appeared in the fat stomach of Overton Avant. It looked like a pin puncture in that mass.

"Oh," said Avant, as he looked down toward the pain. He slowly raised the derringer again, and Blue Steele fired another shot into Avant's guts. Avant sat down in the dirt with a thump. His bulk kept him sitting up straight. His head sagged onto his chest. Blood ran down his white suit from two small punctures in his rotundity.

By this time, Blanch had gotten up onto her hands and knees in the dirt. She stared at the actor in horror and disbelief as he walked toward her, gun in hand. Blue Steele stopped a few feet away from Blanch. He held his pistol pointed at her head. He looked at her for a moment, then he tucked the pistol back under the bib.

"You deserve to die," he said, "but I can't shoot you. To hell with you."

"Who are you?" said Blanch.

Blue Steele took off his soft cap and tossed it aside. Then he pulled off the fake beard and wig of Friedrich Arthur and dropped them in the dirt. He turned to walk toward the bridge. Blanch stared after him in disbelief.

"Abel Kane," said Avant between gasps.

Then Blanch looked at Avant who sat bleeding on the ground. She scrambled over to him and began pulling money out of his pockets. He stared blankly at her, his breaths gurgling. When she had rifled all his pockets, she scrambled for the bills in the dirt that Avant had been trying to retrieve a few moments earlier. Grabbing up the last of the money in sight, Blanch turned back toward the saloon. Overton Avant, with his last bit of strength and his last shot, raised the derringer and put a bullet in her back. She fell on her face, not yet dead, and she struggled to turn and face her killer. Blanch Storey and Overton Avant lay in the dirt of West Riddle, the town they had jointly ruled, and watched each other slowly bleed to death.

CHAPTER NINE

Blue Steele stepped up onto the Missouri River bridge. He had done much killing, and he was suddenly very tired. He had intended to walk across the bridge, but he stopped. He stepped over to the rail and leaned heavily with both hands on it. The dark waters of the mighty Missouri raced beneath him. His role-playing was over. The violence was over. He felt a sense of purposelessness. He had no place left to go. He supposed that he would invent yet another character and move on somewhere.

It had taken Maribel a few moments to recognize Blue. At first he had been not only too far away, but he had also had on the total Friedrich Arthur disguise. When he got up on the bridge without the wig and beard, she had finally known it was him. She broke from her spot just on the other side of the dividing line and ran for Blue.

"Blue," she called. "Blue."

Blue raised his head and looked toward her. He turned and held out his arms, and Maribel ran into them.

"It's all over, Maribel," he said.

"Oh, Blue, are you all right? You're not hurt?"

"I'm all right. Just a little tired."

"Oh, God," she said, "I was so worried about you. And, Blue, there's something you ought to know."

"What's that, Maribel?"

"That man in New York? He's not dead. You didn't kill him. You're not wanted for anything."

Blue stared blankly at Maribel.

"Not dead?" he said. "What—what are you talking about? Chester?"

"I don't know his name, but I read the story in the paper. The New York paper that Mr. Miller got."

"The *Times,*" said Blue. "Yes, I saw that."

"Did you read the story?"

"No. No, I didn't read it."

Blue had lived for so long in the belief that he had murdered Chester that he was having a difficult time getting into his head what Maribel was telling him. He shook his head as if trying to clear it of something. He turned away from Maribel and stared again at the deep waters.

"Well," said Maribel, "he didn't die. The paper said so. Mr. Miller told me first. Then I looked at it and read the story. Blue, you're not wanted for murder."

Blue laughed a short bitter laugh.

"This is really ironic," he said.

"I don't know what that means."

"I thought that I was wanted for murder, and it turns out that I'm not, but here in West Riddle I've just killed so many that I've lost count. Neosho told me to cut notches on my gun butt, but I haven't kept up with it. I'm a killer now, Maribel. There's no mistake about it. Just look down the street."

Maribel's glance followed the sweep of Blue's arm. In her range of vision were the bodies of Avant, Blanch and Gurnsey in the street and that of Chicken still hanging from the roof of the saloon. As she looked, Maribel could see the people of West Riddle beginning slowly to come out of their doors. At the same time the crowd on the other side of the line had started to walk toward Blue and Maribel. They were being led by Coleman Miller and Bluff Luton.

"Blue," she said, "look."

He looked up to see the crowds from both sides of the river closing in on them. *What do they want?* he wondered. *To hang me? Well, let them. I'm too tired to fight them or to run. Besides that, I don't know where I'd run to. To hell with it!*

"Did he get them all?" someone from the Riddle crowd asked.

"Every last damn one," answered someone from West Riddle.

"Really cleaned house."

"By God."

Coleman Miller stepped up and took Blue's hand in both of his, pumping it vigorously.

"Hamlin," he said, "or Steele. Whoever you are. I didn't think that you'd get away with it. I'm glad to see you standing here."

Blue couldn't figure out how to react. He just stood there, a bit dumbfounded. Sergeant Bluff Luton stepped forward and slapped Blue on the shoulder.

"You did a hell of a job over here," he said. "I'm sorry that we couldn't help you out, but, you know, my jurisdiction prevents me from doing anything over here."

"Oh," said Blue, "I wasn't looking for any help. You did turn Avant back for me though."

"We didn't do a damn thing," said Luton. "I don't know what you're talking about."

"Sarge," said Blue, "how's this all going to come out?"

"What do you mean?"

"Well, I know that what I did over here is out of your jurisdiction, but there's bound to be some law for this place."

"Yeah," said Luton, "U.S. marshal. If you can ever get him to come down here."

"What's he going to do to me when he finds out about all this?"

"Not a damn thing," said one of the citizens of West Riddle. "You saved our town."

"Ought to get a damn medal," said another one.

"I killed some people," said Blue. "That's against the law, isn't it?"

"Well," said Luton, "technically, I guess you could be charged with the killings."

"We can't have that," shouted one of the West Riddle citizens.

"We won't let them charge him with nothing. You stay in West Riddle, mister. We'll protect you. Hell, we'll say someone else done all the killing."

Coleman Miller whispered something in the ear of Sergeant Bluff Luton, and Luton nodded approvingly. Then the marshal turned toward the West Riddle crowd.

"You know," he said, "there wouldn't be no questions asked if you had a town marshal and he had cleaned out that bunch."

The citizens turned toward each other and murmured.

"We ain't got a town marshal," said one of them out loud.

"You got a citizens' committee?" asked Luton.

"No."

"This here looks like a citizens' committee to me," Luton continued. "A citizens' committee could appoint a town marshal. Could be the appointment was even made yesterday."

The crowd murmured some more.

"West Riddle needs a good citizens' committee and a good town marshal," said Coleman Miller. "And if I was a citizen of West Riddle, I'd get myself on that committee and I'd vote for Mr. Bluford Steele for town marshal."

Following some more murmuring among the citizenry, Charlie Lewis, the owner of the stable, stepped forward. He walked over to Blue.

"Mr. Steele," he said, "my name is Charlie Lewis. I've just been elected the chairman of the Citizens' Committee of West Riddle, and as such I've been given the authority to appoint a town marshal. I'd like to ask you to accept the appointment. Will you take it?"

Blue looked from Lewis to Maribel. Then he looked at Luton and at Miller. Miller was smiling.

"Take it, Steele," said Luton. "They couldn't get a better man for the job."

"I'm tired of playing roles," said Blue. "Mr. Lewis, do you know that I'm a Cherokee Indian?"

"Didn't know that," said Lewis. "Don't care."

He looked over his shoulder at the rest of his committee. Shoulders were shrugged. Lewis turned back to Blue.

"That don't make no difference to our committee," he said. "Will you take the job?"

"Can you give me just a few minutes?" asked Blue.

"Sure," said Lewis.

Blue took Maribel by the arm and led her back toward the center of the bridge away from the crowd at the West Riddle end. He was thinking about a white woman in New Hampshire and about her father and the good citizens of Hanover. He was thinking about how those people had reacted to the idea of an Indian marrying a white woman.

"Maribel," he said, "what are you going to do now?"

"I don't know, Blue. Mr. Miller said I could stay and work for him if I want to. I don't have any place to go."

"Do you want to stay and work for Miller?"

Maribel shrugged her shoulders.

"I don't have anything else to do," she said.

"Do you think I ought to take that job?"

"Oh, yes. I do, Blue. I think you should take it."

"Maribel," said Blue. He looked down at the bridge and shuffled his feet. He shoved his hands inside the bib of the farmer's overalls he still wore. "Maribel, if I was to take the job and stay in West Riddle . . ."

"Yes, Blue?"

"If I was to take the job and stay in West Riddle, do you think that you might stay, too?"

"What do you mean, Blue?"

"I mean, do you think that you might stay with me? If I take the job?"

"Do you want me to live with you?"

"I want you to marry me, Maribel," said Blue. "Will you?"

"Yes, Blue. I will," she said. She pulled his face down to hers and kissed him full on the lips. When they finally parted, she stood on her toes to look over Blue's shoulder toward the crowd down at the West Riddle end of the bridge.

"Hey," she shouted. "Mr. Lewis. You and your committee. You just got yourselves a new town marshal."

ABOUT THE AUTHOR

Robert J. Conley is a Western writer and editor who specializes in Cherokee lore. He is an associate professor of English at Morningside College in Iowa. He lives in Sioux City, Iowa, and is the author of one previous Double D Western, *Back to Malachi.*